Pleas(

You i

You ca

D0590635

———

12808874

Going Down Slow

John Harvey

Going Down Slow

John Harvey

Five Leaves Publications
www.fiveleaves.co.uk
www.fiveleavesbookshop.co.uk

Going Down Slow

by John Harvey

Limited edition hardback
ISBN 978-1-910170-44-1

Published in 2017
Five Leaves Publications
14a Long Row, Nottingham NG1 2DH
www.fiveleaves.co.uk
www.fiveleavesbookshop.co.uk

The stories were previously published as follows:

"Not Tommy Johnson": *OxCrimes*, ed. M. Ellingham & P. Florence

"Second Chance": *Guilty Parties*, ed. M. Edwards

"Going Down Slow": Random House ebook, reprinted in special
edition Arrow paperback for sale at Sainsbury's, 2014.

"Fedora": *Deadly Pleasures*, ed. M. Edwards. Winner of the CWA
Short Story Dagger, 2014.

"Handy Man": *Ambit* magazine, No 204, Spring 2011

"Ask Me Now": *These Seven*, ed. R. Bradshaw

"Dead Dames Don't Sing": No.32 in the *Bibliomystery Series*,
ed. O. Penzler

Printed in Great Britain

Contents

Not Tommy Johnson   7

Second Chance   17

Going Down Slow   27

Fedora   39

Handy Man   51

Ask Me Now   63

Dead Dames Don't Sing   83

Not Tommy Johnson

Tommy Johnson was not Tommy Johnson. That's to say, he was not the Tommy Johnson whom Resnick first saw skating, perfectly balanced, across the mud of the opposition's penalty area, red hair catching fire for an instant in the floodlights, before dispatching the ball into the upper right corner of the net; the Tommy Johnson who scored forty-seven goals in 118 appearances for Notts before moving on to Derby County, Aston Villa and points north; Resnick's favourite player, amongst other favourite players, in that team that won promotion two seasons running, those brilliant years 1989/90/91 when it seemed they could do little wrong.

The same years that found him struggling still to come to terms with the failure of his marriage, Eileen having sequestered herself somewhere across the Welsh border with her estate agent lover, leaving Resnick custody of four cats, an unused upstairs nursery in which the alphabet wallpaper was already starting to peel, and an overflowing collection of vinyl he was slowly but studiously replacing with CDs — most recently, working alphabetically, Duke Ellington's 1959 score for *Anatomy of a Murder*.

Tommy Johnson's body — that's *this* Tommy Johnson, three weeks and four days past his sixteenth birthday — was found on the uneven paving beneath the fifth-floor balcony from which it had fallen; one arm stretched out at a broken angle, the other wrapped tight across his eyes, as if to ward off any sight of what was fast approaching.

If anyone had heard his helpless cry or the thump of the body landing — landing with sufficient impact to break not only various and sundry bones, but to rupture, also, a number of internal organs — they were, as yet, not saying.

It had been Gerry Clark who'd found him, a little after four in the morning and on his way to the bus that would take him to his job in the distribution centre out by the motorway; just light enough, from the solitary overhead lamp still working, for him to make out the body where it lay, unmoving; what was recognizably blood further darkening the cracks in the paving.

That was two days ago, some forty-eight hours and counting, and Resnick, slightly out of breath after choosing the stairs over the dubious aromas of the lift, was at Danielle Johnson's door; not the first time and likely not the last.

One glance and she turned back into the flat, expecting him to follow. Cotton draw-string pyjama bottoms, sweater, fluffy slippers.

A wall-eyed mongrel barked as he entered, hackles raised, then backed away, growling, from the kick that failed to follow.

Dark in the room, Resnick eased the curtain sideways, letting in a sliver of November light. Opposite him as he sat, Danielle lit a cigarette with a shaky hand and shivered as she inhaled.

'Whatever you or anybody else might've said about him, he never deserved that. Never. Not Tommy. And don't try tellin' me he jumped of his own accord, 'cause I'll not wear it. Someone had it in for him an' that's a fact.'

'Any ideas who?'

She coughed and shook her head; coughed again.

Nine-thirty in the morning and the off-key sweetness of cider on her breath as she spoke; two empty cans, last night's, on the table and a litre bottle, recently opened, on the floor nearby. Not long past thirty, Danielle: three kids who'd been in and out of care; Tommy the only boy, her favourite. Melody, the youngest, living with her nan now in Derby; Janine in temporary foster care in another part of the city.

'You saw him that evening?' Resnick asked.

Danielle fanned smoke away from her face. 'In and out. Nine it might've been. Later, maybe.'

'Any idea where he was going?'

She shook her head. 'Not his keeper, am I? Ask, he'd only tell me, mind me own fuckin' business.'

'So you don't know who he might have been seeing that evening?'

'Just said, never told me anything.'

'It's important, Danielle.'

'I know it's fuckin' important. Think I'm fuckin' stupid?'

The first thoughts of those who'd responded to the emergency call, the police, the paramedics: Tommy Johnson had taken his own life, jumped to his death under the influence, most likely, of this, that or the other. Something more than self-pity. But a small trace of cannabis aside, that and paracetamol, there were no drugs, untoward, in his body, and all he seemed to have drunk in the twenty-four hours previous, water aside, was a copious quantity of Red Bull.

An examination showed blows to the head and body quite possibly administered prior to the injuries sustained in his fall. Another homicide the last thing the team wanted — Tommy's especially — but it was, it seemed, what they were getting.

Officers went to the school in theory he'd attended; having been excluded so many times, since September-end he'd more or less excluded himself. They talked to the few from around the estate who would admit to having spent any significant time with him; talked to the social worker who'd been attached to him since his last brief spell in care.

Quiet, pretty much a loner. Bit of a loser, really.

'No great loss to humanity, I'm afraid,' his Citizenship teacher had said.

After another twenty minutes or so of getting nowhere, Resnick rose to his feet and Danielle prised herself out of the settee and saw him to the door. When he was halfway to the stairs, she called him back.

'There was this girl he was keen on. Leah? Leah something. Felix, maybe? Skirt up to her arse an' a mouth to match.'

Resnick had spent so long working in close proximity with a fellow officer who thought Petula Clark's *Greatest Hits* the acme of all things musical, it had been something of a shock to discover someone else in the force with a feeling for jazz. Tom Whitemore was a member of the Public Protection Team: working with other agencies — probation, social services and community psychiatric care — in the supervision of violent and high risk of harm offenders released back into the community, sex offenders in particular.

As was often the case, it was older relatives who'd passed the jazz torch from one generation to another: with Resnick it had been an uncle, amongst whose scratched 78s he had discovered Billie Holiday and Teddy Wilson, and through them, Johnny Hodges and Lester Young; Whitemore's father had made him a present of Cannonball Adderley's *The Dirty Blues* for his sixteenth birthday. Whether he would as easily be able to do the same for his twin boys depended on the good grace of his estranged wife and her new partner. One way and another, the job took its toll.

When Resnick arrived at the Five Ways, towards the end of the first set, a scratch band, in which he recognised only Geoff Pearson on bass, was bustling through Coltrane's "Blue Train" with at least half an eye on the interval.

'Leah Felix,' Resnick said, once they'd removed themselves to the side bar, 'any bells?'

Whitemore, he knew, had for some months now been involved in unpicking a complicated and as-yet-unproven case of sexual exploitation, in which a closely-knit group of men had groomed a number of young teenage girls, for the most part living in care. The girls had been talked into posing for explicit photographs which had been shared over the internet; after which, and with more persuasion, the girls themselves had been shared between the members of the group and their friends. Loaned out, sometimes, in order to pay off debts.

Leah Felix had been one of the more reluctant, hesitant about going along with the others and submitting to the men's suggestions. Once the police and social services became involved, she had seemed one of the most likely to name names, be prepared, even, to give evidence in court. But when push had come within sight of shove, she had clammed up and backed away.

Whitemore told Resnick what he knew.

'You think she might talk to me?'

'What about?'

10

'Tommy Johnson.'

'The footballer?'

Resnick shook his head.

He located Leah Felix amidst a small group that had congregated at the edge of the Old Market Square: smoking roll-ups, taking selfies, swearing at anyone who came close. Only the promise of a Quarter Pounder with cheese, onion rings and fries could prise her away; that and the assurance he'd keep his hands to himself. 'I know what you old blokes are like, given half a chance.'

The nearest McDonald's was on Exchange Walk, with a view across to St. Peter's Church.

Resnick waited until she was halfway through her burger, wondering, as he watched her, when she'd last had a proper meal.

'Tommy Johnson, he was a friend of yours.'

'Was he?'

'So his mum says.'

'Danielle? That slag.'

'Is she right, though?'

Leah shrugged and jammed a few more fries into her mouth.

'You know what happened to him?' Resnick asked.

'Jumped off fuckin' balcony, didn't he? Daft twat.'

'No, I mean what really happened.'

She looked at him then. Blinked.

'You do know?'

'Dunno what you're on about.'

'I thought you did.'

'Well, I fuckin' don't.'

Resnick reached out and purloined a chip. 'She thought you might've been with him that evening.'

'Who?'

'Danielle.'

'Fuckin' out of it, most the time, in't she?'

'That mean she was wrong?'

'Maybe. Maybe not. An' stop takin' my fuckin' fries.'

'You were with him, then?'

11

'So what if I was?'

'He liked you, didn't he? Tommy. Liked you quite a lot.'

'Did he?'

'I think so.'

'Know everything then, don't you?' She pushed away her tray and made as if to get up.

'Wait,' Resnick said.

She hesitated, then sat back down.

'If you were with him that evening,' Resnick said, 'you must have seen what happened.'

'Well, I never did.'

Her eyes flicked towards him then away. Resnick bided his time.

'I… I wanted to. Go with 'em, like, you know? Thought if I was there they wouldn't hurt him. Not so bad, anyway. But they never let me. Told me to fuck off out of it an' keep my mouth fuckin' shut.'

'Why were they going to hurt him?'

'Been shootin' his mouth off, yeah? Tellin' them to leave me alone. Like they'd listen, right? Threatened if I wouldn't shop 'em to you lot then he would. Stupid bastard. Soft in the bloody head.'

'So who was it?' Resnick asked. 'Took Tommy away?'

'Don't be stupid.'

'All right, how many. You can tell me that. Just a number. That's all it is.'

Uncertain, the answer was slow in coming. 'Three. No, four. Four.'

'And the names?'

'No. No way.'

'One of them, then. Just one.'

'No. No, I can't.' There was panic in her eyes.

'All right, then. We'll do it like this.' From his pocket he took a sheet of paper, folded twice. Written on it were the names of a dozen men Whitemore was investigating. 'Just point to the names of whoever went off with Tommy that evening. That's all I'll ask. And no one will ever need to know. I promise.'

The polish on Leah's index finger was chipped and cracked; the nail itself bitten down to the quick. She jabbed at the names so quickly, scarcely touching the paper, that Resnick had to ask her to do it again, more slowly.

'They said… they promised… ' She turned her head aside, lest he see the tears pricking at the corners of her eyes. She wasn't gonna fuckin' cry, not in front of some fuckin' copper she wasn't.

Resnick showed Tom Whitemore the names.

'Who's the most vulnerable?' he asked. 'Who's got the most to lose?'

Lewis Morland was older than the rest by a good ten years; it didn't mean he was wiser, just more cunning. Now that his once-boyish good looks were fading and his age beginning to show, he'd started befriending young girls on Tumblr and ASKfm, feigning the identity of an eighteen-year-old. Out on the street, he was dependent on others to make the first moves.

Previous convictions meant that if he went back inside it would be for a long and uncomfortable time.

Resnick and Whitemore interviewed him together, Morland slippery as a grass snake in their hands, a combination of 'No comment', *non sequiturs* and ingratiating smiles.

'Tommy Johnson? Not that bloke used to play for Notts? Never saw him myself, but my old man reckoned he was the dog's bollocks.'

None of the others Leah Felix had fingered would admit to coming within a mile of where the incident had occurred.

'Think maybe she was playing safe?' Whitemore said. 'Feeding us the wrong names?'

'It's possible,' Resnick replied.

But he had seen her face, recognised her fear. For the present, he preferred to believe.

A little over three weeks later, the Low Copy Number DNA test results on Tommy Johnson's clothing came back from the special research lab in Birmingham. Aside from Johnson's own blood, present in generous quantities, initial tests had revealed small amounts of blood from two other possible sources; after re-examination, one of these, when checked against the National DNA Database, was sufficient to identify Marshall Boyce.

13

Boyce, a seventeen-year-old with a minor police record, had been on Tom Whitemore's list, but not picked out by Leah Felix.

Resnick found Leah in Sun Valley Amusements in the city centre.

Her eyes narrowed the moment she saw him, fingers clenched into tight little fists. 'You said you was never gonna say nothin', din't you?'

'I kept my word.'

'Then how come Lewis had a go at me, yeah? Gave me a right slapping.'

There was still the faint trace of what could have been a bruise, just visible beneath her make-up.

'You want to file a complaint?'

'Fuck off!'

'The names — why didn't you tell me the truth?'

'I did.'

'Not all the truth.'

'What d'you mean?'

But she knew well enough.

'Marshall Boyce, you were in care round about the same time.'

'So?'

'So you know him. Better maybe than the others. Soft spot for him, maybe.'

She shrugged.

'Is that why you didn't pick him out?'

She squinted up her eyes. 'Gotta fag?'

Resnick shook his head. She bummed one from someone by the adjacent slot machine and Resnick followed her outside.

'He was always, like, decent, you know, Marshall. When the others, like Lewis especially, when they wanted to do really dirty stuff, porno stuff, he never went along with it. Not usually, anyway. Tried to talk 'em out of it, till they called him a poof an' that an' then he stopped.'

'We know he was there when Tommy was killed,' Resnick said.

'What d'you need me for, then?'

'Corroboration.'

'What's that?'

14

Unlike Lewis Morland, in the formality of the interview room, faced with two senior officers, Marshall Boyce folded like a discarded hand of cards. They'd just been going to give a Tommy a kicking, he said, learn him to keep his nose out of things as didn't concern him. Only Tommy, 'stead of running, he started to fight back. Caught Marshall one in the face and he had to get him back for that, didn't he? All of 'em laying into him and Tommy, he was leaning back against the wall, lashing out and crying. Marshall was all for letting it be, but Lewis he said, no, teach the little fucker a lesson once and for all. And that was when Tommy scrambled up onto the wall and next you know he'd gone.

'He jumped,' Resnick said. 'Is that what you're saying? Or did he fall? How did it happen?'

Marshall closed his eyes as if remembering.

'Just for this minute, right, he was standing there, staring at us, and then his arms, they started waving like crazy, like he was losing his balance, right? And then he must've gone over backwards, 'cause it was just like suddenly he weren't there.'

'Nobody pushed him?' Resnick asked, a moment later.

Marshall shook his head. 'Nobody had to.'

He made a statement testifying to the names of the others who were present, detailing the part they'd played in the proceedings. All five were arrested and charged with Tommy Johnson's murder. Before it came to trial the CPS might decide to drop the charge down to manslaughter; a persuasive brief might get it lowered further, causing grievous bodily harm, say, but Resnick thought that unlikely.

Several weeks after the men had been remanded into custody, he came face to face with Leah Felix in the Old Market Square and she turned and walked off in another direction. That evening he phoned Tom Whitemore to see if he was planning on going to the Five Ways, but there was no answer. On the way home, he picked up some Polish sausage and potato salad, remembering at the last moment he was low on cat food; too late this evening to get along to the West End Arcade and Music Inn, his CD project now at the end of the Es, Gil Evans: *New Bottle Old Wine*.

Still there was always tomorrow: another day.

Another day for some. Not Tommy Johnson.

Second Chance

He hadn't recognised her. Not right off. A slender woman in blue jeans and a green parka hesitating on the pavement outside the building where he lived. Her hair scraped back into a tight pony tail; make-up an afterthought at best.

'Jack...'

'Victoria?'

It had been the voice that had nailed it, Essex laid through with pre-teen years of elocution lessons, a mother with ideas above her station. Basildon, at the time, east from London on the line to Shoeburyness.

'I thought this was the right address, but then, with the shop and everything, I wasn't sure.'

For the past several years, home for Jack Kiley had been a first-floor flat above a charity shop in north London, the stretch of road that led from Tufnell Park down towards Kentish Town. Terry, that morning's volunteer, drape jacket and duck tail, was playing Chuck Berry at near full volume. Midway through the guitar solo on 'Johnny B. Goode', the needle stuck and was lifted delicately clear and set back down a beat before the voice returned.

'You hungry?' Kiley asked.

She shook her head.

'Coffee, then?'

'Okay.'

He threaded her through the lines of buses and private cars to the Vietnamese café across the street. One latté, a flat white, and, for Kiley, a baguette with chillies, coriander and garlic pork.

'Breakfast, Jack, or lunch?'

'Both?'

When she smiled, crow's feet etched deeper around her eyes.

He had first met her when she was just nineteen, a minor sensation at Wimbledon and on her way to being something of a celebrity: Victoria Clarke, the first British woman to reach the semi-finals since Boudicca, or so it had seemed. Her world ranking had been twenty-three and rising; in the *Observer* list of *Britain's Top 20 Sportswomen*, she was number seven with a bullet. Canny, her agent had bartered her image between cosmetic companies and fashion houses, settling finally for a figure that tripled whatever she was likely to make out on the WTA tour.

During the Championships, billboards appeared in every major city, showing Victoria in full-colour action: crouching at the base line, racket in hand, lips slightly parted, waiting to receive; watching the high toss of the ball, back arched, white cotton top taut across her breasts. Beneath both, the same strap line: *A Little Honest Sweat!* The deodorant itself was pictured discreetly bottom right, alongside the product's name.

Students tore them down and used them to paper their rooms. Feminists festooned them with paint. Victoria crashed out in the semis 6-1 and 6-0, came unstuck in the first round the following year; three years on, advertising contract cancelled, she failed to get through qualifying. Retired at twenty-five.

Since then, she'd done a little coaching, some tennis commentary on local radio, moved for a while to Florida — more coaching — and returned the wiser. The last time Kiley had caught sight of her, aimlessly flicking the remote, she had been modelling heart-shaped pendants on *The Jewellery Channel*.

'So, how's it going?' he asked.

'You know…' Shrug of the shoulders, toss of the hair.

'You're looking good anyway.'

'And you're a lousy liar.'

Kiley bit down into his baguette; a touch of chilli but not too much. 'When you called, you just said you needed to see me. You didn't say why.'

'I was probably too embarrassed.'

'And now?'

She curled the ends of her hair around her finger, sipped her latté.

'I always seem to be coming to you with my problems, Jack.'

'Goes with the job,' Kiley said.

Victoria had fallen pregnant when she was fifteen and persuaded her older sister to bring the child up as her own; an unorthodox way of parenting that had threatened to break into the spotlight just when her big advertising contract was due to be signed. One of Kiley's first jobs as a private detective, having some time previously resigned from the police, had been to trace the root of the problem; help it go away.

'This isn't about Alicia?'

'No. Not at all.'

'So tell me.'

She leaned closer; lowered her voice. 'When I was in the States I met this man, this guy. Adam. He wasn't American, English, he was out there filming. Some, I don't know, documentary. We... we had this, this thing. I suppose it was pretty intense for a while.' She lifted her cup; set it back down. 'Anyway, he came back, I stayed. We kept in touch, you know, phone calls, email. It was okay for a while, but then he started getting on at me, trying to get me to change my mind. About living there. Come back to England, he'd say. We had something special, didn't we? It's not as if what you're doing is going anywhere. And he was right, that was the thing, I suppose I just didn't like being told. As if I'd made, you know, another mistake. But in the end — he wore me down, I suppose — I packed it all in, what I was doing, the coaching, and came back, and then when I saw him again there was nothing. A big zero. Nothing. It wasn't just I didn't fancy him, Jack, I didn't even like him.'

'And I suppose he didn't feel the same?'

A quick shake of the head. 'When I told him, tried to tell him, he wouldn't listen. Went on and on about how he'd made all these plans, put his life on hold, while all the time I'd been leading him on. I tried to reason with him but he just went — I don't know — crazy. Called me every dirty name under the sun. Punched the wall. The wall, Jack.'

'Not you? He didn't hit you?'

'No, though I think it came close. In the end he calmed down enough to tell me he never wanted to set eyes on me again. If he did, he didn't know what he might do.' She straightened, arching her neck. 'That was a little over a year ago.'

'And now?'

Victoria sighed, twiddled more hair. 'When we were… when I was still in Florida, some of the emails we sent, back and forth, they were… they were pretty, well…'

'Sexy?'

'Yes. Just, you know, what would you do if I were there now? What would you like me to do? That sort of thing. Pretty harmless, really. But then, after a while, there was more. More than just, you know, words.'

'Photos? Videos?'

'Yes.' Not looking, looking away, out towards the plate glass of the window, the road. Her voice was dry, small. 'There was a camera on the laptop. He'd make up these little scenes and have me act them out. Download them and then edit them. Send them back. Some of them, they were…'

Her voice trailed into silence.

Outside, the driver of a Murphy's construction lorry was embroiled in a noisy argument with a cyclist in full gear, padded shorts, skin-tight top, helmet, the whole bit.

'You want anything else, Jack?' the young Vietnamese woman who ran the café asked.

'No, thanks,' Kiley said, 'I think we're fine.'

Victoria opened her smartphone, went into her emails and passed the phone across the table. Time enough for Kiley to see the image of a naked shoulder; a woman, clearly Victoria, turning her face towards the camera, the open bed behind; when the image disappeared, a message: *Listen up, whore. Less you want this all over the internet, do like I say.*

'That's it?' Kiley asked.

'A couple more, the same. Just threats. Nothing spelled out. And then a few days ago another, asking for money. Stupid money.'

'And these emails, they came from the same address?'

'All except the most recent, yes. But any reply bounces back, un-deliverable, account closed.'

'And the one asking for money, how're you supposed to pay?'

'It doesn't say.'

Kiley thought he could do with another flat white after all.

'It's someone playing around,' he said. 'Someone's idea of a joke.'

'It's no joke, Jack, especially not now. Not when I'm just starting to turn things around. I've got a shot as a presenter for one thing, only on one of the shopping channels, but it's a start. And I've been talking to BT Sport about maybe doing Wimbledon next year; you know, expert analysis, that sort of thing, other tournaments, too. All it needs is for that stuff to get out onto the internet and for the media to get hold of it, and I wave all of that goodbye. Besides which, there's Alicia. Think what it might do to her.'

Kiley followed her out on to the street.

'She's staying with me now, Jack, term time at least.'

'How come?'

'I arranged with Cathy for her to switch schools last September. Year Eight, Jack, can you imagine that? Alicia, all grown up.'

'And your sister, she's okay with that?'

'She and Trevor, they've been going through a bad patch, and if I'm to be honest, I think Alicia's part of the reason. I think it'll do them good to spend some time without her.'

'Alicia, she's happy about it, too?'

Victoria looked at him in surprise. 'Of course. I am her mother, after all.'

People are rarely, if ever, what you expect. Adam Lucas was shortish — five-five at best — and stockily built; gingerish hair cropped short on top and a trim goatee showing the first signs of grey. Kiley tried to picture him together with Victoria and failed. But then, what did people think when he was out with Kate, when she introduced him to her friends? Her aberration? Her bit of rough? An experiment in social engineering?

Lucas Film's offices were in a basement in Soho, Bateman Street, two rooms liberally festooned with posters: a documentary about illegal migrant workers in East Anglia; a short film about embalming; a recent London Film Festival poster for *Bad Monkey: Carl Hiaasen's Crazy World*, showing grinning alligators deep amongst the everglades.

There was a receptionist's desk, but no receptionist. Adam Lucas was editing something on a laptop. He shook Kiley's hand, looked twice at his card.

'This for real?'

'Real as it gets.'

'Never say that to a maker of documentaries.'

There was a low settee along a side wall; all the easier, Kiley thought, for Lucas's feet to touch the floor. Petty, but he enjoyed it nonetheless.

'How about pornography?' Kiley asked.

Lucas looked at him askew. 'Not something we're involved in.'

'Just privately.'

'Sorry?'

'Yesterday, I was talking to Victoria.'

'I don't understand.'

'Little home movies she made in Florida. Your direction. Do this, do that, put that there. Someone's threatening to put them on YouTube, Viddler, Phanfare.'

'And you think that's me?'

'Until you convince me otherwise.'

Lucas shook his head, reached for a cigarette. 'I haven't seen Vicky in twelve months, more. Haven't called, emailed, anything. It's — whatever it was — it's over, finished. Last year's model. She made that clear enough.'

'All accounts, you were pretty angry when she did.'

'She'd fucked me around, of course I was angry.'

'And this is a way of getting your own back.'

Tilting back his head, Lucas let a slow stream of smoke waver up towards the ceiling.

'Tell you something about myself, Jack. It is Jack? I've got a short temper, short fuse. Always have. Got me in trouble at school and just about every day since. But once it's blown it's blown. People I work with, they understand.

'Vicky walked in here now, I'd kiss her on both cheeks, shake her hand. No grudges, Jack. Believe it.'

Kiley thought maybe he did.

'These films, videos, whatever, if they were just private between the two of you…'

'How could someone else have got access?'

'Yes.'

'They're not exactly sitting around on my hard drive, waiting for someone to hit on them by chance. Okay, I could've been hacked into, it happens all the time, but then, so could she.'

Lucas got to his feet.

'I can't help you, Jack. Wish I could. See Vicky, give her my love. And those videos, believe me, compared to what's out there, it's pretty tame stuff. I'd tell her to chill out, whoever it is, call their bluff.'

Since returning from America, Victoria Clarke had been living south of the river, Clapham, a nest of Edwardian terraces between Lavender Hill and the Common. Kiley could hear the commotion from the front door. A young voice raised in anger, words scything the air: 'bitch', 'selfish cow', 'bitch' again. Footsteps and the sound of something breaking, smashed against the floor. Helplessness on Victoria's face; helplessness mixed with resignation. Behind her, feet stamping up stairs and then the slamming of a door.

'Hormones,' Victoria said, ruefully. 'Kicking in a little early in Alicia's case.'

Kiley followed her along a narrow hallway and into a living room with French windows out into the garden. Flowers in a glass vase above the fireplace. Tail fuzzed out, a black and white cat scuttled out the moment they walked in.

'Belongs two doors down,' Victoria explained. 'Sneaks in here whenever she gets the chance. Sleeps on Alicia's bed, more often than not.' She smiled. 'Calming influence, cats, or so they say.'

'What was all the shouting about anyway?'

'Oh, she wanted to have some friends round for a sleepover next weekend. From her new school. Three of them. I said I thought three was too many.'

She sat down and gestured for Kiley to do the same.

'She'll stay angry for an hour or so, shut herself in her room. I'll back down a little, compromise on two friends instead of three. It'll be fine.'

Kiley told her about his meeting with Adam Lucas.

Bass prominent, the sound of music from above filtered down.

'Have there been any more emails?' Kiley asked.

Victoria shook her head.

'Maybe it was just someone messing around. Came across one of the videos somehow and decided to chance their arm.'

'I don't see how that could happen.'

'Me neither. But what I don't understand about the internet would fill a large book.'

What Kiley didn't understand, almost certainly Colin Baddeley did. Something of an IT whiz and briefly attached to the Met, which was where Kiley had first met him, Baddeley now had a very nice and expensive line in electronic surveillance. For friends, he was usually prepared to throw in a little pro bono after hours.

A lover of real ale and British folk music — the two interests irreducibly yoked together — Kiley took him round a generous supply of Baltic Porter from Camden Town Brewery and a copy of Shirley Collins' *The Sweet Primroses* he'd found knocking around at the back of the charity shop.

'These emails she's been getting,' Kiley said, 'is there any way of finding out where they're from?'

It took Baddeley something in the region of ten minutes. From the IP address to the ISP in a matter of moments and from there he was able to access the right geolocation: general area, region, post code. Satellite picture on the screen.

'I owe you,' Kiley said.

Baddeley nodded in the direction of his newly acquired and rare L.P. 'I'd say, paid in full.'

He had to ring the bell three times before Alicia came to the door. A One Direction T-shirt over pink pyjama bottoms.

'Mum's out.'

'I know. It's not your mum I've come to see.'

Her room was at the top of the house; a view out through dormer windows towards the Common. Kiley lifted a bundle of clothing off the one comfortable-looking chair and set it carefully down; other clothes were scattered haphazardly across the floor. Alicia was sitting cross-legged on her bed, chewing on a length of hair. The computer was on a table against the far wall.

'Why?' Kiley asked.

A small shrug of the shoulders, avoiding his eyes.

'Tell me,' Kiley said.

'So you can tell her.'

'No. So you can tell her yourself.'

'As if.'

He let it pass. Watched. Waited. She hated being stared at, he could see that, hated the silence, the expectation.

It didn't last.

'She was really stupid, right. Thinking just 'cause she'd deleted all that stuff it wouldn't still be there, on the hard drive, somewhere. And, besides, she's got this Time Machine, right, backs up everything. Automatic. I mean, what did she think?'

'She might have thought you'd respect her privacy.'

'Joking, right? Respect. She's spreading her legs for some bloke on camera an' I'm s'posed to show her respect.'

'She is your mum.'

'An' that's s'posed to make it better.'

'No. No, it's not.'

'I hate her.'

'You don't.'

'I do. I fuckin' hate her. Makin' me come an' live down here and go to this crappy school, 'stead of being with my mates. Just 'cause she's decided, after all this time, she wants to play fuckin' mum. Wanted to do that, she should've done it when I was born, instead of givin' me away.'

There were tears in her eyes, the words choking from her throat.

Kiley wanted to go across and give her a hug, but stayed where he was.

Waited.

'You need to talk to her about it,' he said.

'Oh, yeah, right.'

25

'No, really, you should. Maybe get someone else to help.'

'What, like some counsellor?'

'Maybe. If that's what it needs.'

Alicia sniffed, wiped a hand across her face. Twelve going on fifteen. Twelve going on seven.

Slowly, Kiley got to his feet. 'No more emails, eh? No more threats.'
Alicia followed him downstairs.

'Your mum would have made me a cup of tea,' he said in the hall.

'Yeah, well, I'm not my mum, am I?'

Not yet, Kiley thought. 'You'll tell her I called,' he said.

'Maybe,' Alicia said. ''Less I forget.'

She was grinning as she closed the door.

Going Down Slow

When they first began living together, himself and Lynn, Resnick would be woken by dreams of her dying; his fear of losing her transformed into violent imaginings from which he would wake slick with sweat, to find her laying there beside him, peacefully sleeping. Only then could he rest, assured that she was still breathing. And with time the dreams faded, became less frequent, less frightening, though they never disappeared entirely: and never once in his dreams did he see how she would really die.

When eventually it came, it was sudden, and if there were a blessing to be found, he supposed that was it. The suddenness. A moment of realisation, of pain, perhaps not even that, then nothing. No time for goodbyes.

He thought of this later, those long slow afternoons when he would sit by his friend Peter Waites' bed, patiently waiting for him to die. But in the weeks, the months following Lynn's death no such rationalisation was possible.

At home, he prowled from room to room, the house suddenly over-large, alien; refusing to sleep in the bed they'd shared, he spent broken nights in an armchair, blanket pulled across his knees, listening to Monk's discordant threnodies, Billie's anguished love songs, chippy and forlorn: familiar music he barely recognised or really heard.

At work — the Central Police Station in the city centre, divisional HQ — he blundered from floor to floor, office to office, most eyes turning away from him, awkward, uncomfortable, as soon as he came near, fellow officers embarrassed by his grief; a few older colleagues alone finding words of sympathy, reaching out to squeeze his shoulder, his hand.

Near to retirement, the task of running the robbery division pulled out from beneath him, as far as the job was concerned he was a dead man walking. 'No call for you to be here at all,' the divisional commander told him, 'not when you're due compassionate leave. And counselling, Charlie, someone to talk to, professional, that's what you need.'

Only one person he wanted to talk to and she was dead.

Karen Shields, a detective chief inspector from the Homicide and Serious Crime Command in the Met, had been brought in to run the investigation into Lynn's murder. The local force would be offering her all the assistance it could. She was careful to speak to Resnick early on, express her condolences, glean from him whatever she deemed useful, give assurances that she would keep him informed of whatever progress was being made.

Was it because she was a woman she'd been chosen, Resnick had wondered? Some strange politically correct equivalence? But then he had quickly realised it was because she was a good detective, good at her job. He kept out of her way as much as he could.

For a time, he found himself farmed out to B Division in the north of the county, providing cover for senior officers absent through illness and accident. His journey there took him past a succession of neatly grassed-over slag heaps, cosmetic testimony to an industry that had once employed thousands; an uncomfortable reminder of when he had been running an intelligence-gathering team during the Miners' Strike, feeding back information that had contributed to the government decimating the coal fields and bringing the union to its knees. At the time, he had been able to convince himself he was playing his part in preventing the country being rent asunder by civil disorder. Now, with each new revelation prised from previously secret Cabinet archives, he felt that, along with many others, he had been manipulated, used, taken for a ride.

One of the few good things, for Resnick, to have come out of that time had been the unlikely friendship he had formed with one of the most outspoken of the striking miners, Peter Waites: a friendship built on mutual respect that had come close to floundering when

Waites' son, Jack, had opted to join the police and, for a time, had been stationed in Nottingham under Resnick's command. But Jack Waites had decided soon enough police work was not for him, and decamped to Australia, a wife, kids and a successful career in IT.

Resnick and Peter Waites had taken to meeting every month or so in Waites' local in Bledwell Vale, and when that closed down through lack of patronage — the village itself now more or less deserted — in whatever pub they could find in Bolsover or Chesterfield that served a decent pint and didn't have TV screens in every corner of the bar.

It was here that Resnick first heard of Waites' nephew, Ryan, Ryan Lessings, recently sentenced to eighteen months for stealing goods from the cash and carry where he'd been working and selling them on eBay.

'Everything from maxi-packs of breakfast bloody cereal to digital radios. Needs his brains tested, the idiot. Not the first time, neither. Let him off with a fine he could never pay an' community service, whatever the hell that is. His missus warned him if it happened again, she'd up sticks and leave him to it. Likely will an' all. Mind of her own, Melanie, though when she hooked up with Ryan she must've had it switched into reverse.'

'Kids?' Resnick asked.

'Just the one. Lassie, four year old. Emma. Not the brightest. Learning difficulties, that what they call it nowadays?'

Resnick thought perhaps it was. Seeing Waites' glass was all but empty, he lifted it up with his own and headed for the bar. Just the one more, then time to head back down the motorway to where the cat would be waiting, patient, to be fed.

Time passed. For one reason or another, the two men failed to meet up for six months or more, and before they did see one another again, Lynn's killer had been found, a youth with little more motive on his mind than to take vengeance for a perceived wrong and gain the respect of his own father in the process.

'A waste, Charlie,' Peter Waites said when they did meet. 'A sad bloody waste.'

At first Resnick took him to mean Lynn, before realising he meant the lad as well. Not so very many years on, Resnick thought, the same youth would be released and still have years ahead of him to make a life; not so Lynn.

'Hard for you to see it that way,' Waites said. 'For now, any road.'

Resnick nodded and supped his pint.

'That hapless nephew of mine,' Waites said. 'Ryan bloody Lessings. Kicking him free end of the month. Served just over half his time. Back out on the street with what he stands up in an' not a deal more. Melanie, she and the kiddie upped sticks like she said. Place down in Nottingham. Your way, Mapperley Top. One of them houses broke down into flats.'

'She'll have him back?'

'Like hell she will.'

'Any other family? Close?'

'Not as'd give him house room. Drove his old lady, my sister Mary, to an early grave as it is. No one else'll speak to him but me, and if you do offer him a mote o'kindness all he does is throw it back in your face.'

'You'll not be inviting him back to the Vale, then?' Resnick said with a smile. 'Stay with you a while?'

Waites made a face. 'Not thank me if I did. Hostel, that's the best he can hope for. For now, at least.'

'And Melanie? She can manage on her own?'

'Benefits, she'll just about cope. An' once kiddie's off to school proper, she can likely find work, part-time.'

'He'll not go bothering her? Ryan?'

'Likely get short shrift if he does.'

Just weeks later Resnick was back at Divisional HQ, notionally babysitting new recruits to CID, ignoring best as he could the know-it-all-already looks on their smooth-skinned faces.

Free for a while from his charges, he was whiling away the time talking soccer with Jamie Wood, the two of them standing by Wood's Ford Estate in the parking area to the rear of the police station when the call came through: a domestic out at Mapperley called in by neighbours. Windows broken and worse. Wood switched on the in-car laptop and checked for details.

'Like company?' Resnick asked.

Wood shrugged: why not?

Ryan Lessing was pacing up and down the broken-flag pathway, criss-crossing the square of stubbled grass, words flailing like angry birds aimless from his mouth. Behind the windows of the narrow brick-built house, curtains were closed; two of the ground-floor windows cracked across.

Wood drew the vehicle over towards the kerb, Resnick exiting before it had come to a true stop. Calling Ryan Lessing's name.

He turned sharply towards them, Skrewdriver T-shirt loose over his jeans; dark hair cut close to the scalp, tattoos on his neck, the back of one hand.

Three paces towards Resnick, fist raised, he stopped, seeing Wood approaching from the other side of the car.

'That bitch,' he said, glancing back towards the house, 'she called you, didn't she? Won't let me see my own kid.'

'Ryan,' Resnick said, 'why don't we just calm down?'

'And why don't you bugger off and mind your own business?'

Jamie Wood was close enough now to grab his arm and spin him round, the arm quickly levered up high behind his back, forcing him down onto his knees, head pressed to the ground.

'What d'you think?' Wood said. 'Time for a little quiet rest and contemplation?'

When Resnick knocked on the front door it opened on the chain; ID checked, it closed and opened again. Melanie Lessing stood in the hallway, the ghost of prettiness hovered about her, anxiety startling her eyes.

A small girl, fair-haired — Emma — stared up at Resnick from behind her mother's legs, one hand clinging to the fabric of her worn blue jeans.

'You both okay?' Resnick asked.

Melanie shivered involuntarily. 'Why don't you shut the door?'

They sat in a room crowded with mis-matched furniture, Melanie smoking a cigarette, wafting the smoke away from her daughter's face as the girl sat close by her, still clutching at her leg. Ryan had come round earlier, wanting see his daughter. Hammered on the door,

31

threatening to break it down, tried to force his way in. Melanie had talked to him, stood her ground, tried to reason; told him she'd call the police if he didn't go away and leave them alone. Ryan had lost his temper totally, called her everything under the sun. Wandered off and when he came back he'd been drinking. Thrown God-knows-what at the windows. Threatened more. Now he was sitting in the back of a police car, handcuffed, sullen.

'What will happen?' Melanie asked.

'To Ryan?'

She nodded.

'It depends.'

She took a deep drag at her cigarette, smoke in her lungs.

'Did he hit you?' Resnick asked.

'Not this time.'

'But he has before?'

A shrug of the shoulders, looking back at him with grey eyes. What did he think?

'Isn't there some kind of — what is it? — restraining order?' she said. 'Something that will mean he can't come round and do this again.'

'You can apply for one, yes. Temporary at first, while the court decides whether or not to make it permanent.'

'Mummy,' Emma said quietly. 'When's Daddy coming back?'

The next few times Resnick rang Peter Waites there was no answer. He thought about driving up there to make sure he was okay, but somehow other things kept getting in the way. It was a phone call from Jack Waites in Melbourne that alerted him: his father had been taken into hospital and Jack himself had only just found out. Could Resnick maybe go and see him, call back and let him know how he was?

He could.

He found Waites standing beneath the portico at the hospital entrance, still attached to his portable IV stand, smoking a cigarette.

'Down't pit since I were fifteen, Charlie, coal dust enough on my lungs to bank half fires in bloody Bolsover. I doubt a John Player Special or two's gonna make a scrap of difference. Not now, any road.'

He had stage three cancer: a tumour of over seven centimetres in his right lung and busily spreading into the layers covering the heart.

'I'll let Jack know,' Resnick said. 'He'll want to come over.'

'Best get a shift on or all he'll be in time for's bloody funeral.'

Waites turned his head aside and coughed up black phlegm into the palm of his hand.

But when Jack arrived, four days later, the situation seemed to have, if not radically improved, levelled out at least. The drugs seemed to be working; the spread of the cancer all but halted. His father well able to sit up in bed and talk, take himself off to the bathroom without assistance, sneak the odd cigarette or two and joke about it with the nurses afterwards.

Jack stayed the best part of a week, frequently texting home, texting work, sitting hunched over his laptop beside his father's bed or hunkered down in a corner of the hospital canteen. The IT firm he worked for were in the midst of a possible takeover and there was only so much he could do at a distance. And he needed to stay involved.

'Don't you fret yoursen,' Peter Waites said. 'There's life in the old sod yet.'

Neither father nor son were sure they would see one another again.

Melanie Lessing's application for a restraining order against her husband was successful, the court issuing an injunction prohibiting him from coming within an agreed distance of her home address, and from attempting to contact her or their daughter without prior arrangement. After one month, if this injunction were adhered to, Ryan would be able to spend time with his daughter — once a week initially — under social service supervision.

Out that way on routine business, Resnick called at the house: an early spring day, crocuses just showing in the scrap of garden, the sun still shallow in the sky. In the cramped living room Melanie was working her way through a pile of ironing, television playing aimlessly in the background. Some of the lines seemed to have smoothed from her face; blonde highlights in her hair.

She greeted Resnick with a smile. 'This is where I put kettle on, is it?'

'I'll not say no.'

On the screen a once well-known actor was selling incontinence products for over-sixties. Resnick looked away.

'Fresh out of biscuits, I'm afraid. Emma took the last Jammie Dodger with her to nursery.'

'How is she?'

'She's fine. Loves nursery. Never wants to come away.'

'And her dad?'

'Missed a session with Emma — when? — last week, the week before. But that aside...' Reaching out, she touched her fingers to the wood of the chair. '... okay. Not been round here, anyway, bugging me.'

'New leaf, then. Seen the error of his ways.'

'You believe that?'

'Happens.'

'Not Ryan. Should've seen it years ago and never did, not till it was too late. Good on promises, Ryan. Least, he used to be. Things he was going to do, we were both going to do, places we'd go. Australia, he'd say, like Jack. Why not, nothing for us here.' Setting her mug of tea on the floor, she reached for a cigarette. 'He was right enough there.'

Peter Waites' condition suddenly worsened. A second tumour, malignant, forming in the fluid around the heart. After consultation, a decision was taken to cease all further treatment and manage the pain. A place was found in a hospice close to Mansfield offering specialist palliative care. Visiting, Resnick realised Waites had never really looked ill before: now he did.

No strength in his hand; little warmth.

A flicker in the eyes.

'A bugger, eh, Charlie?'

Resnick nodded agreement.

After a very few minutes more, Waites closed his eyes and slept.

Resnick waited, went out into the corridor, back to the reception area, bought tea and a caramel wafer from one of the volunteer helpers, took them back.

He found one of the nurses, black with a Mansfield accent and weave in her hair, grandparents who likely came over on the Windrush in response to the Health Service cry of need.

'What are we looking at?' Resnick asked. 'Weeks or… ?'

'Weeks would be good. In a case like your friend's, weeks would be unusual.'

When he went back into the room again, Waites was awake and staring at the TV set anchored to the far wall.

'Your lad…' Resnick began.

'No.'

'How d'you mean?'

'You'll not tell him.'

'He'll want to know.'

'And what? See me like this? Sit there watchin' me croak?'

'It's his right.'

'Is it hell! Besides, time he booked a flight, made it over…' He let the rest of the sentence hang. 'When he was here before I wasn't too bad. I don't want him to see me like this.'

'Even so…'

'No, Charlie, no.' He gripped Resnick's hand then with what little strength he had. 'You've got to promise me, Charlie. Promise, right. The funeral, that'll be time enough.'

The effort brought on a fit of coughing and Resnick levered him carefully forward, gave him water to sip through a straw, and rested him back down as gently as he could.

Early evening, two days later, and Resnick was pottering about the kitchen, nibbling on ends of hard cheese while trying to ignore the cat winding between his legs pretending it hadn't already been fed. He didn't hear the phone straight away, over the sound of Ellington's "Harlem Air Shaft", playing loud in the other room.

Jamie Wood's voice was curt and urgent. 'Melanie Lessing. I'll meet you there.'

The front door to the house was splintered and had been knocked sideways off its hinges. The door to the flat, veneered MDF, kicked through. Melanie stood in the middle of the living room, cigarette in one hand, another burning in an ash tray. Save for the blood seeping from an unsealed cut high on her forehead, all trace of colour had drained from her face.

'Ryan?'

She nodded. 'It's Emma. He took her.'

'Took her how?'

'Grabbed hold of her. Screaming. Threw her over his shoulder. He had a car. Pushed her in the back and drove off.'

'This was when?'

'I don't know... fifteen minutes gone, twenty... whenever I phoned.'

'And the car?'

She shook her head. 'Not big. Ordinary.'

'Colour?'

'Grey. That sort of silvery-grey.'

'How about the make? D'you know the make?'

Another shake of the head. 'It could have been... I don't know... It could have been a Vauxhall... I don't know why.'

'And the number? I don't suppose you got the number?'

'I tried. CY, I noticed that... a 7 at the end.'

'You're sure?'

'Yes, I think so.'

Jamie Wood stepped outside, speaking into his mobile.

Resnick took the last inch of smouldering cigarette from Melanie's fingers and stubbed it out. Her eyes were wild.

'Sit yourself down.'

'I can't.'

'You can.' He eased her into a chair. 'My turn to make the tea.'

'I don't want no fucking tea!'

'I'll put kettle on just the same.'

There were traffic cameras at all the main junctions, CCTV, peppered along the major routes in and out of the city. Silver-grey saloon, possibly a Vauxhall, most likely an Astra, similar shape; partial number plate; one adult male driving. Car itself most likely stolen and recently.

'You wait here, Charlie,' Wood said. 'Might think twice and double back, you never know. I'll get myself down to Central. Keep you informed.'

Resnick made tea and brought it through. Dabbed the cut on Melanie's head clean, applied a plaster. After a while, she went into the bedroom and came back with a scrapbook, pictures of Emma as a baby.

'She'll be all right,' Resnick said.

'Will she? You read about it all the time, don't you? Men killing their wives and children. Children, especially. If I can't have you, no one else can. Cowards, that's all they are.'

'This isn't like that,' Resnick said.

He didn't know.

Dark settled around the windows, shrouding the houses across the street, the low wall, the patch of garden beyond the front door. Resnick didn't want to think of Lynn, of Lynn dying, but he did. Two shots from close range as she stepped through the gate on her way towards the house, the end of a journey she would never complete, would never make. Kneeling beside her on the grass, breathing life into her dead body, her blood warm in his mouth.

His mobile rang.

Jamie Wood.

A Vauxhall Astra answering the description had been sighted, a short distance past the Greyhound Stadium on the A612, the edge of Colwick Wood.

'Best you stay here,' Resnick said, as he ended the call.

'I'm coming.'

'Best not.'

She wasn't listening. There was an old suit he'd been meaning to drop off at the cleaner's on the passenger seat and he threw it into the back to make room.

They arrived moments after Jamie Wood, two other response vehicles immediately behind. The car stood on the edge of shadow, illuminated now by police headlights. A body lay slumped over the steering wheel, unmoving.

'This time you do wait,' Resnick said. 'No argument.'

Solemn-faced, Melanie nodded agreement. Bit down into her lip, piercing skin.

Resnick followed Jamie Wood forward. Stood beside him as he wrenched open the car door.

Ryan Lessing had swallowed the contents of a bottle of pain killers and then, to make sure, slashed his throat with a Stanley knife: there was a great deal of blood.

Turning away, Wood called for someone to phone for an ambulance, but it was a formality at best.

There was no sign of anyone else in the car.

No child.

'She's got to be somewhere,' Wood said, glancing off towards the trees.

Stepping round to the back of the car, Resnick snapped open the boot.

Emma lay there, knees drawn up towards her chest, head down, unmoving.

His breath stopped in his throat.

'Emma?'

Nothing.

'Emma?'

Slowly, she uncurled, face turning towards the light.

Thanks to his diminishing duties, Resnick was able to visit the hospice for an hour or more each day; sit alongside Peter Waites' bed, making desultory conversation, sitting more often in silence broken only by the low hum of machinery, the outcrop of occasional dreams. Waites leaning suddenly forward, propelled by memory, the shout of 'Scab!' from his parched mouth a rusted echo of its former self. 'Maggie, Maggie, Maggie! Out, Out, Out!' The fingers of one hand struggling to make a fist.

'You've not called him?' he asked, abruptly waking. 'Jack.'

'I've not.'

For four days it was the truth, difficult for his conscience to assuage: on the fifth, a day on which Waites barely stirred, he finally phoned. 'You'd best come. He's fading fast.'

The first flight available, via Dubai, thirty hours, give or take, door to door.

Jack Waites would have been passing over the Egyptian coast when his father died. Resnick only registering, some little time after it had happened, that his friend's breathing had stopped.

The room suddenly airless: deadened.

Resnick sat there, unmoving; reached out and touched, for a moment, the back of Peter Waites' hand, and, leaning forward, kissed him on the forehead, once.

Then went to call the nurse.

Fedora

When they had first met, amused by his occupation, Kate had sent him copies of Hammett and Chandler, two neat piles of paperbacks, bubble-wrapped, courier-delivered. A note: *If you're going to do, do it right. Fedora follows.* He hadn't been certain exactly what a fedora was.

Jack Kiley, private investigator. Security work of all kinds undertaken. Ex-Metropolitan Police.

Most of his assignments came from bigger security firms, PR agencies with clients in need of baby-sitting, steering clear of trouble; solicitors after witness confirmation, a little dirt. If it didn't make him rich, most months it paid the rent: a second-floor flat above a charity shop in north London, Tufnell Park. He still didn't have a hat.

Till now.

One of the volunteers in the shop had taken it in. 'An admirer, Jack, is that what it is?'

There was a card attached to the outside of the box: *Chris Ruocco of London, Bespoke Tailoring.* It hadn't come far. A quarter mile, at most. Kiley had paused often enough outside the shop, coveting suits in the window he could ill afford.

But this was a broad-brimmed felt hat, not quite black. Midnight blue? He tried it on for size. More or less a perfect fit.

There was a note sticking up from the band: on one side, a quote from Chandler; on the other a message: *Ozone, tomorrow. 11am?* Both in Kate Keenan's hand.

He took the hat back off and placed it on the table alongside his mobile phone. Had half a mind to call her and decline. Thanks, but no thanks. Make some excuse. Drop the fedora back at Ruocco's next time he caught the overground from Kentish Town.

41

It had been six months now since he and Kate had last met, the première of a new Turkish-Albanian film to which she'd been invited, Kiley leaving halfway through and consoling himself with several large whiskies in the cinema bar. When Kate had finally emerged, preoccupied by the piece she was going to write for her column in the *Independent*, something praising the film's mysterious grandeur, its uncompromising pessimism — the phrases already forming inside her head — Kiley's sarcastic 'Got better, did it?' precipitated a row which ended on the street outside with her calling him a hopeless philistine and Kiley suggesting she take whatever pretentious arty crap she was going to write for her bloody newspaper and shove it.

Since then, silence.

Now what was this? A peace offering? Something more?

Kiley shook his head. Was he really going to put himself through all that again? Kate's companion. Cramped evenings in some tiny theatre upstairs, less room for his knees than the North End at Leyton Orient; standing for what seemed like hours, watching others genuflect before the banality of some Turner Prize winner; another mind-numbing lecture at the British Library; brilliant meals at Moro or the River Café on Kate's expense account; great sex.

Well, thought Kiley, nothing was perfect.

Ozone, or to give it its proper title, Ozone Coffee Roasters, was on a side street close by Old Street Station. In full view in the basement, industrial-size roasting machines had their way with carefully harvested beans from the best single-estate coffee farms in the world — Kiley had Googled the place before leaving — while upstairs smart young people sat either side of a long counter or at heavy wooden tables, most of them busy at their laptops as their flat whites or espressos grew cold around them. Not that Kiley had anything against a good flat white — a twenty-first century man, or so he sometimes liked to think, he could navigate his way round the coffee houses in London with the best of them.

Chalked on a slate at the front of one of the tables was Kate Keenan's name and a time, 11:00, but no Kate to be seen.

Just time to reassess, change his mind.

Kiley slid along the bench seat and gave his order to a waitress who seemed to be wearing mostly tattoos. Five minutes later, Kate arrived.

She was wearing a long, loose crepe coat that swayed around her as she walked; black trousers, a white shirt, soft leather bag slung over one shoulder. Her dark hair was cut short, shorter than he remembered, taking an extra shine from the lighting overhead. As she approached the table her face broke into a smile. She looked, Kiley thought, allowing himself the odd ageist indiscretion, lovelier than any forty-four-year-old woman had the right.

'Jack, you could at least have worn the hat.'

'Saving it for a special occasion.'

'You mean this isn't one?'

'We'll see.'

She kissed him on the mouth.

'I'm famished,' she said. 'You going to eat?'

'I don't know.'

'The food's good. Very good.'

There was an omelette on the menu, the cost, Kiley reckoned, of a meal at McDonald's or Subway for a family of five. When it came it was fat and delicious, stuffed with spinach, shallots and red pepper and bright with the taste of fresh chillis. Kate had poached eggs on sourdough toast with portobello mushrooms. She'd scarcely punctured the first egg when she got down to it.

'Jack, a favour.'

He paused with his fork halfway to his mouth.

'Graeme Fisher, mean anything to you?'

'Vaguely.' He didn't know how or in what connection.

'Photographer, big in the sixties. Bailey, Duffy, Fisher. The big three, according to some. Fashion, that was his thing. Everyone's thing. *Biba*. *Vogue*. You couldn't open a magazine, look at a hoarding without one of his pictures staring back at you.' She took a sip from her espresso. 'He disappeared for a while in the eighties — early seventies, eighties. Australia, maybe, I'm not sure. Resurfaced with a show at Victoria Miro, new work, quite a bit different. Cooler, more detached: buildings, interiors, mostly empty. Very few people.'

Skip the art history, Kiley thought, this is leading where?

'I did a profile of him for the *Independent on Sunday*,' Kate said. 'Liked him. Self-deprecating, almost humble. Genuine.'

'What's he done?' Kiley asked.

'Nothing.'

'But he is in some kind of trouble?'

'Maybe.'

'Shenanigans.'

'Sorry?'

'Someone else's wife; someone else's son, daughter. What used to be called indiscretions. Now it's something more serious.'

Following the high-profile arrests of several prominent media personalities, accused of a variety of sexual offences dating back up to forty years, reports to the police of historic rape and serious sexual abuse had increased four-fold. Men — it was mostly men — who had enjoyed both the spotlight and the supposed sexual liberation of the sixties and later were contacting their lawyers, setting up damage limitation exercises, quaking in their shoes.

'You've still got contacts in the Met, haven't you, Jack?'

'A few.'

'I thought if there was anyone you knew — Operation Yewtree, is that what it's called? — I thought you might be able to have a word on the quiet, find out if Fisher was one of the people they were taking an interest in.'

'Should they be?'

'No. No.'

'Because if they're not, the minute I mention his name, they're going to be all over him like flies.'

Kate cut away a small piece of toast, added mushroom, a smidgeon of egg. 'Maybe there's another way.'

Kiley said nothing.

As if forgetting she'd changed the style, Kate smoothed a hand across her forehead to brush away a strand of hair. 'When he was what? Twenty-nine? Thirty? He had this relationship with a girl, a model.'

Kiley nodded, sensing where this was going.

'She was young,' Kate said. 'Fifteen. Fifteen when it started.'

'Fifteen,' Kiley said quietly.

'It wasn't aggressive, wasn't in any sense against her will, it was… like I say, it was a relationship, a proper relationship. It wasn't even secret. People knew.'

'People?'

'In the business. Friends. They were an item.'

'And that made it okay? An item?'

'Jack…'

'What?'

'Don't prejudge. And stop repeating everything I say.'

Kiley chased a last mouthful of spinach around his plate. The waitress with the tattoos stopped by their table to ask if there was anything else they wanted and Kate sent her on her way.

'He's afraid of her,' Kate said. 'Afraid she'll go to the police herself.'

'Why now?'

'It's in the air, Jack. You read the papers, watch the news. Cleaning out the Augean stables doesn't come into it.'

Kiley was tempted to look at his watch: ten minutes without Kate making a reference he failed to understand. Maybe fifteen. 'A proper relationship, isn't that what you said?'

'It ended badly. She didn't want to accept things had run their course. Made it difficult. When it became clear he wasn't going to change his mind, she attempted suicide.'

'Pills?'

Kate nodded. 'It was all hushed up at the time. Back then, that was still possible.'

'And now he's terrified it'll all come out…'

'Go and talk to him, Jack. Do that at least. I think you'll like him.'

Liking him, Kiley knew, would be neither here nor there, a hindrance at best.

There was a bookshop specialising in fashion and photography on Charing Cross Road. Claire de Rouen. Kiley had walked past there a hundred times without ever going in. Two narrow flights of stairs and then an interior slightly larger than the average bathroom.

Books floor to ceiling, wall to wall. There was a catalogue from Fisher's show at Victoria Miro, alongside a fat retrospective, several inches thick. Most of the photographs, the early ones, were in glossy black and white. Beautiful young women slumming in fashionable clothes: standing, arms aloft, in a bomb site, dripping with costume jewellery and furs; laughing outside Tubby Isaac's Jellied Eel Stall at Spitalfields; stretched out along a coster's barrow, legs kicking high in the air. One picture that Kiley kept flicking back to, a thin-hipped, almost waif-like girl standing, marooned, in an empty swimming pool, naked save for a pair of skimpy pants and gold bangles snaking up both arms, a gold necklace hanging down between her breasts. Lisa Arnold. Kate had told him her name. Lisa. He wondered if this were her.

The house was between Ladbroke Grove and Notting Hill, not so far from the Portobello Road. Flat-fronted, once grand, paint beginning to flake away round the windows on the upper floors. Slabs of York stone leading, uneven, to the front door. Three bells. Graeme Fisher lived on the ground floor.

He took his time responding.

White hair fell in wisps around his ears; several days since he'd shaved. Corduroy trousers, collarless shirt, cardigan wrongly buttoned, slippers on his feet.

'You'll be Kate's friend.'

Kiley nodded and held out his hand.

The grip was firm enough, though when he walked it was slow, more of a shuffle, with a pronounced tilt to one side.

'Better come through here.'

Here was a large room towards the back of the house, now dining room and kitchen combined. A short line of servants' bells, polished brass, was still attached to the wall close by the door.

Fisher sat at the scrubbed oak table and waited for Kiley to do the same.

'Bought this place for a song in sixty-four. All divided up since then, rented out. Investment banker and his lady friend on the top floor — when they're not down at his place in Dorset. Bloke above

46

us, something in the social media.' He said it as if it were a particularly nasty disease. 'Keeps the bailiffs from the sodding door.'

There were photographs, framed, on the far wall. A street scene, deserted, muted colours, late afternoon light. An open-top truck, its sides bright red, driving away up a dusty road, fields to either side. Café tables in bright sunshine, crowded, lively, in the corner of a square; then the same tables, towards evening, empty save for an old man, head down, sleeping. Set a little to one side, two near-abstracts, sharp angles, flat planes.

'Costa Rica,' Fisher said, 'seventy-two. On assignment. Never bloody used. Too fucking arty by half.'

He made tea, brought it to the table in plain white mugs, added two sugars to his own and then, after a moment's thought, a third.

'Tell me about Lisa,' Kiley said.

Fisher laughed, no shred of humour. 'You don't have the time.'

'It ended badly,' Kate said.'

'It always ends fucking badly.' He coughed, a rasp low in the throat, turning his head aside.

'And you think she might be harbouring a grudge?'

'Harbouring? Who knows? Life of her own. Kids. Grandkids by now, most like. Doubt she gives me a second thought, one year's end to the next.'

'Then why... ?'

'This woman a couple of days back, right? Lisa's age. There she is on TV, evening news. Some bloke, some third-rate comedian, French-kissed her in the back of a taxi when she was fifteen, copped a feel. Now she's reckoning sexual assault. Poor bastard's picture all over the papers. Paedophile. That's not a fucking paedophile.' He shook his head. 'I'd sooner bloody die.'

Kiley cushioned his mug in both hands. 'Why don't you talk to her? Make sure?'

Fisher smiled. 'A while back, round the time I met Kate, I was going to have this show, Victoria Miro, first one in ages, and I thought, Lisa, I'll give her a bell. See if she might, you know, come along. Last minute, I couldn't, couldn't do it. I sent her a note instead, invitation to the private view. Never replied, never came.'

He wiped a hand across his mouth, finished his tea.

'You'll go see her? Kate said you would. Just help me rest easy.' He laughed. 'Too much tension, not good for the heart.'

Google Maps said the London Borough of Haringey, estate agents called it Muswell Hill. A street of Arts and Crafts houses, nestled together, white louvred shutters at the windows, prettily painted doors. She was tall, taller than Kiley had expected, hair pulled back off her face, little make-up; tunic top, skinny jeans. He could still see the girl who'd stood in the empty pool through the lines that ran from the corners of her mouth and eyes.

'Lisa Arnold?'

'Not for thirty years.'

'Jack Kiley.' He held out a hand. 'An old friend of yours asked me to stop by.'

'An old friend?'

'Yes.'

'Then he should have told you it's Collins. Lisa Collins.' She still didn't take his hand and Kiley let it fall back by his side.

'This old friend, he have a name?' But, of course, she knew. 'You better come in,' she said. 'Just mind the mess in the hall.'

Kiley stepped around a miniature pram, various dolls, a wooden puzzle, skittles, soft toys.

'Grandkids,' she explained, 'two of them, Tuesdays and Thursday mornings, Wednesday afternoons. Run me ragged.'

Two small rooms had been knocked through to give a view of the garden: flowering shrubs, a small fruit tree, more toys on the lawn.

Lisa Collins sat in a wing-backed chair, motioning Kiley to the settee. There were paintings on the wall, watercolours; no photographs other than a cluster of family pictures above the fireplace. Two narrow bookcases; rugs on polished boards; dried flowers. It was difficult to believe she was over sixty years old.

'How is Graeme?'

Kiley shrugged. 'He seemed okay. Not brilliant, maybe, but okay.'

'You're not really a friend, are you?'

'No?'

48

'Graeme doesn't do friends.'

'Maybe he's changed.'

She looked beyond Kiley towards the window, distracted by the shadow of someone passing along the street outside.

'You don't smoke, I suppose?'

'Afraid not.'

'No. Well, in that case, you'll have to join me in a glass of wine. And don't say no.'

'I wasn't about to.'

'White okay?'

'White's fine.'

She left the room and he heard the fridge door open and close; the glasses were tissue-thin, tinged with green; the wine grassy, cold.

'All this hoo-hah going on,' she said. 'people digging up the past, I'd been half-expecting someone doorstepping me on the way to Budgens.' She gave a little laugh. 'Me and my shopping trolley. Some reporter or other. Expecting me to dig up the dirt, spill the beans.'

Kiley said nothing.

'That's what he's worried about, isn't it? After all this time, the big exposé, shit hitting the fan.'

'Yes.'

'That invitation he sent me, the private view. I should have gone.'

'Why didn't you?'

'I was afraid.'

'What of?'

'Seeing him again. After all this time. Afraid what it would do to all this.' She gestured round the room, the two rooms. 'Afraid it could blow it all apart.'

'It could do that?'

'Oh, yes.' She drank some wine and set the glass carefully back down. 'People said it was just a phase. Too young, you know, like in the song? Too young to know. You'll snap out of it, they said, the other girls. Get away, move on, get a life of your own. Cradle snatcher, they'd say to Graeme, and laugh.'

Shaking her head, she smiled.

'Four years we were together. Four years. Say it like that, it doesn't seem so long.' She shook her head again. 'A lifetime, that's what it was. When it started I was just a kid and then…'

She was seeing something Kiley couldn't see; as if, for a moment, he were no longer there.

'I knew — I wasn't stupid — I knew it wasn't going to last forever, I even forced it a bit myself, looking back, but then, when it happened, I don't know, I suppose I sort of fell apart.'

She reached for her glass.

'What's that they say? Whatever doesn't kill you, makes you strong. Having your stomach pumped out, that helps, too. Didn't want to do that again in a hurry, I can tell you. And thanks to Graeme, I had contacts, a portfolio, I could work. David Bailey, round knocking at the door. Brian bloody Duffy. *Harper's Bazaar*. I had a life. A good one. Still have.'

Still holding the wine glass, she got to her feet.

'You can tell Graeme, I don't regret a thing. Tell him I love him, the old bastard. But now…' A glance at her watch. '… Mr Collins — that's that I call him — Mr Collins will be home soon. Golf widow, that's me. Stops him getting under my feet, I suppose.'

She walked Kiley to the door.

'There was someone sniffing round. Oh, a good month ago now. More. Some journalist or other. That piece by Kate Moss had just been in the news. How when she was getting started she used to feel awkward, posing, you know, half-naked. Nude. Not feeling able to say no. Wanted to know, the reporter, had I ever felt exploited? Back then. Fifteen, she said, it's very young after all. I told her I'd felt fine. Asked her to leave, hello and goodbye. Might have been the *Telegraph*, I'm not sure.'

She shook Kiley's hand.

When he was crossing the street she called after him. 'Don't forget, give Graeme my love.'

The article appeared a week later, eight pages stripped across the Sunday magazine, accompanied by a hefty news item in the main paper. ***Art or Exploitation?*** Ballet dancers and fashion models, a few gymnasts and tennis players thrown in for good measure. Unhealthy relationships between fathers and daughters, young girls and their coaches or mentors. The swimming pool shot of Lisa was there, along with several others. Snatched from somewhere, a recent picture of Graeme Fisher, looking old, startled.

'The bastards,' Kate said, vehemently. 'The bastards.'

Your profession, Kiley thought, biting back the words.

They were on their way to Amsterdam, Kate there to cover the re-opening of the Stedelijk Museum after nine years of renovations, Kiley invited along as his reward for services rendered. 'Three days in Amsterdam, Jack. What's not to like?'

At her insistence, he'd worn the hat.

They were staying at a small but smart hotel on the Prinsengracht Canal, theirs one of the quiet rooms at the back, looking out onto a small square. For old times sake, she insisted on taking him for breakfast, the first morning, to the art deco Café Americain in the Amsterdam American Hotel.

'First time I ever came here, Jack, to Amsterdam, this is where we stayed.'

He didn't ask.

The news from England, a bright 12-point on her iPad, erased the smile from her face: as a result of recent revelations in the media, officers from Operation Yewtree yesterday made two arrests; others were expected.

'Fisher?' Kiley asked.

She shook her head. 'Not yet.' When she tried to reach him on her mobile, there was no reply.

'Maybe he'll be okay,' Kiley said.

'Let's hope,' Kate said, and pushed back her chair, signalling it was time to go. Whatever was happening back in England, there was nothing they could do.

From the outside, Kiley thought, the new extension to the Stedelijk looked like a giant bathtub on stilts; inside didn't get much better. Kate seemed to be enthralled.

Kiley found the café, pulled out the copy of *The Glass Key* he'd taken the precaution of stuffing into his pocket, and read. Instead of getting better, as the story progressed things went from bad to worse, the hero chasing round in ever-widening circles, only pausing, every now and then, to get punched in the face.

'Fantastic!' Kate said, a good couple of hours later. 'Just amazing.'

There was a restaurant some friends had suggested they try for dinner, Le Hollandais; Kate wanted to go back to the hotel first, write up her notes, rest a little, change.

In the room, she switched on the TV to catch the news. Over her shoulder, Kiley thought he recognised the street in Ladbroke Grove. Officers from the Metropolitan Police arriving at the residence of former photographer, Graeme Fisher, wishing to question him with regard to allegations of historic sexual abuse, found Fisher hanging from a light flex at the rear of the house. Despite efforts by para-medics and ambulance staff to revive him, he was pronounced dead at the scene.

A sound, somewhere between a gasp and a sob, broke from Kate's throat and when Kiley went across to comfort her, she shrugged him off.

There would be no dinner, Le Hollandais or elsewhere.

When she came out of the bathroom, Kate used her laptop to book the next available flight, ordered a taxi, rang down to reception to explain.

Kiley walked to the window and stood there, looking out across the square. Already the light was starting to change. Two runners loped by in breathless conversation, then an elderly woman walking her dog, then no one. The tables outside the café at right angles to the hotel were empty, save for an old man, head down, sleeping. Behind him, Kate moved, business-like, around the room, readying their departure, her reflection picked out, ghost-like, in the glass. When Kiley looked back towards the tables, the old man had gone.

Handy Man

It was his hands I noticed first. Really took in. Broad, dependable hands. A ring on the wedding finger, dull gold. And the nails, surprisingly even, rounded, no snags, not bitten down; no callouses on the fingers, such as you might expect from a working man, a man who worked with his hands. Only the suggestion of hard skin around the base of the thumb, hard yet smooth.

Harry.

A simple name. Straightforward, simple.

The things I knew about him later: time he'd spent in the army, Northern Ireland, Iraq. Things he would never really talk about, just hints, nightmares, dreams. His anger. Not so simple really. Harry.

Nine years I'd been living in the house then, the first time I set eyes on him. Nine years since the divorce and then all that business with Victor, and I suppose it's true to say for the last two or three years I'd let things go. Easy enough to do when you're living on your own. The cupboard door that won't open without a tug, and once the handle's snapped off, won't open at all; the window that's permanently stuck; the shower that leaks; the wardrobe rail that keeps collapsing under the weight of all too few clothes.

I must have mentioned something to Marie over lunch, just as a way of making conversation, the way things seemed to be falling apart. The second Tuesday of each month, that's when we meet. Years now. The Yacht Club, where she's a member, or the Blue Bell down by the river. Every month, save for November when she and Gerald go off to their timeshare in Florida, and, recently, June, which, these days, they tend to spend with their daughter and her family somewhere near Lake Garda. Otherwise, it's a nice white wine, not too dry, chicken escalopes, pumpkin risotto or Dover sole, and then rather too much of Gerald's progress, greasing his way up the slippery pole of investment banking. Although, to be fair, she's been quieter on that front of late. What we've had are the grandchildren instead. First words, first steps, potty training disasters that are meant to elicit laughter, photos of chubby faces, each, to me, indistinguishable from the other. Isn't he gorgeous? Isn't she lovely?

I do my best, I really do. Make an effort to show some interest, manifest concern. Marie is my best friend, after all. Just about the only one I still have since all the hoo-ha of the divorce, the dirt that Squeegeed out onto the front page of the local paper. What kind of a woman is it who argues for financial parity over the custody of the children? A woman who was clearly no better than she should be, that's what. A husband's long-term adultery with his secretary more acceptable than a wife's dalliances with a PR client on a jolly to Cap d'Antibes. All of that before Victor had slithered onto the scene.

And so because she's stuck with me all this time, I do try, between the crème brulée and the coffee, to share Marie's delight in her burgeoning family. But children, other people's children, I've always found it hard to warm to, and where grandchildren are concerned, well, I'm just not ready. I mean, I am, of course. Chronologically, biologically — but mentally…

It's one of the great advantages of marrying early, Marie says, not like so many women today, you have your grandchildren when you're young enough to enjoy them. Maybe. But there are other things I feel young enough to enjoy and they don't include a return to nappy changing or singing 'Baa-Baa Black Sheep' for the umpteenth time.

Which led, I suppose, to Victor, a black sheep if ever there was one, though a wolf in sheep's clothing.

And then to Harry. Poor Harry.

'What you need,' Marie told me solemnly, after yet another report of some small domestic malfunction, 'is a handy man.' Straight-faced, not a trace of innuendo. 'Here, look…' And from her bag she took a business card, not new, turned down a little at the corners.

CARPENTER/HANDY MAN
Shelves, doors, locks, windows, floors.
Good work, friendly service.
Estimates free.
References available.
Harry Campbell

'We've used him once or twice,' Marie said, 'just for little things. Not too expensive, I'll say that for him. Turns up when he says he will, too. Not like some. And quiet. All I could do to drag a word out of him.' She smiled. 'Tea with milk, no sugar. You could do worse.'

I started fishing around for something to write down the phone number, make a note of the email, but Marie said to keep the card, so I slipped it into my bag and that's where it lay for quite a while. Until one afternoon when I pulled hard at the cutlery drawer and the whole front came away in my hand.

All I got at first was an automated message on his answer phone; then when he called back that evening I was just onto my second glass of wine and settling down to watch Kenneth Branagh in something Swedish and bracing.

'Mrs Francis? It's Harry Campbell. I'm not disturbing you? It's not too late to call?'

His voice was a trifle slow, but sure; traces of an accent I found hard to place.

'No. No, Harry, it's not too late.'

Harry. First name terms from the start. For me, at least. He would continue to call me Mrs Francis for quite some little time.

Eight o'clock, he'd said, and there he was on the doorstep, true to his word. Brown cord jacket and denim shirt, grey-green trousers — chinos I suppose they were; canvas tool bag slung over his shoulder, grey van parked on the street behind. Broad-shoulder, tall. Imposing, is that the word?

'I'm not too early?'
'No, no. Not at all.'

I hadn't quite finished dressing when he rang the bell; the wretched zip on my skirt had stuck, not for the first time, and I'd scarcely had time to run a brush through my hair. Standing there, I fastened another button on my blouse before stepping back to let him in.

'You'd like a cup of tea, I dare say?'

He'd set his bag down in the middle of the kitchen floor.

'No, you're all right for now, thanks. Maybe in a while.'

I hadn't been meaning to stare.

'Something about a busted drawer?' he said. 'A few other things that needed sorting?'

I showed him what required attention and left him to it for the best part of an hour. Made the bed, fixed my face, watered the plants and riffled through the pages of a magazine. A voice I didn't recognise burbled away between songs on Radio 2. The *Telegraph* still lay, folded and unopened, on the table in the hall.

'How about that cup of tea?' I said.

He was stretched out on the floor, ratcheting something underneath the sink.

Slowly, his head eased back into sight. 'Thanks. Just a drop of milk and...'

'... and no sugar.'

'That's right.' When he smiled, the skin crinkled around his eyes.

'I would offer you a biscuit, but...'

'It's okay.' He patted the flat of his stomach. 'Got to watch the weight.'

The cup seemed so small in his hand I thought it must break.

'I suppose you're kept busy,' I said aimlessly, unable to sit there saying nothing.

'Busy enough.'

His eyes were pale blue; his hair, quite wiry, was starting a little prematurely to go grey. I supposed it was prematurely. He was what? Late-thirties, forty, little more. Not so great a gap. His other hand, on the breakfast bar, rested innocently close to mine.

'These units,' he said, glancing round, 'I'll do what I can, but it's a bit like, you know, shifting the deck chairs on the Titanic.'

'You mean we're going to drown?'

'In a manner of speaking.'

Kate Winslet, I thought. Leonardo DiCaprio. Little more than a boy.

'You could get them replaced. Ikea. B&Q. Needn't be expensive, if you don't want.'

'I don't know. This place, I'm not sure how much longer I'm going to stay.'

'Well, just a thought.' He set down his cup and was quickly to his feet. 'Thanks for the tea.'

'You've not finished already?'

'Good as. I'll sweep up those shavings if you've a dustpan and brush.'

'Only I was wondering…'

He looked at me then, waiting.

'The shower, upstairs, it's been leaking. Quite badly now.'

'Seal's gone I dare say, needs replacing. I'll take a quick look, but I've not got the right stuff with me now.' He glanced at his watch. 'I could probably drop back later.'

'Yes, all right. Do. I mean, if that's okay with you.'

It was raining hard when he returned. A darkening across the shoulders of his jacket and, as he came into the hall, careful to wipe his feet, a few drops fell onto his face from where they'd caught in his hair and I wanted to wipe them away.

Desperate Housewives, I thought. I was in danger of becoming a cliché.

The next time he came, a week or so later, I was careful to make myself scarce, dropping a set of keys into his hand the minute he arrived and asking him to pop them back through the letter box when he was through.

'Off to work, then?'

'Something like that.'

The one good thing that came from my distant divorce, as long as I avoided undue extravagance and was careful to tread within my means, there was no more need for nine to five, not regularly at least. The occasional bit of market research, filling in from time to time at the agency where I used to be employed, and that was enough.

So instead I loitered over a latté and Danish at the local coffee franchise, gave over some time to a manicure and polish change; finally took a stroll down by the river, just as far as where they're starting to fill in one of the old gravel pits, turn it into a country park.

As I neared home I tried to ignore the soft flutterings in my stomach, the lingering hope that he would still be there. In his stead, he had left some catalogues showing various styles of kitchen cabinet, appropriate pages turned down.

I stowed them in the bottom of a drawer. Pushed Harry to the back of my mind. Even flirted momentarily, crazily, with the idea of getting back in touch with Victor. One stupid, desperate day I even got as far as the door of the club — part bar, part casino — where he used to spend much of his time.

'Victor? No, he's still away, I think. Out of the country. But if you want to leave a name?'

I shook my head and turned away, legs unsteady as I walked back to my car. Nothing — no promise of pleasure, however strong, however intense — could make me want to go through all of that again. Better by far to stay home with a good book, something comforting on the TV, Valium and a large G & T. The fleeting fantasy of a working man's hands.

Just a few mornings later, as I left the house, my breath caught in my throat; across the street, at the wheel of an almost brand new Merc, window wound down, cuff of his white shirt turned back just so, sat Victor. Victor Sedalis. Smiling.

I should have walked away as if weren't there; gone back inside and locked the door. I continued to stand there like a fool instead.

'I hear you've been looking for me,' he said.

'No.'

'A couple of days ago. Wanting to welcome me back home.'

'I don't think so.'

An eyebrow rose in that sceptical, amused expression I knew so well. 'All right,' he said, 'but you will.' He slid the car into gear. 'Either that or I'll come looking for you.'

I had to lean back against the door and grip my arms hard to stop myself from shaking. Right from the first, there had been something about him that had made me squirm, made me crawl; something that had made it impossible for me to say no. The loans asked for so casually and never returned; the three in the morning phone calls after the club was closed, when he would come to me with cigarette smoke in his hair, brandy on his breath and another woman's perfume on his skin, and still I could never turn him away.

But then, without warning, he disappeared. Minorca, some said, Porte Ventura. Cyprus. Spain. Money he owed, gambling debts that had been gambled again and lost — something shady, dangerous, under-hand. Of course, he had gone off before, weeks, months sometimes. But this seemed more definite, complete.

I floundered, came close to falling apart. It took an overdose and months of psychotherapy, but with help, I put myself back together, bit by bit.

It wasn't going to happen again.

I called Harry and left a message on his machine: one or two things, I said, in need of your attention. The wardrobe, the chest of drawers.

When he arrived, I was busy in the kitchen; a wave and a few quick words and, tool bag over his shoulder, he was on his way up to the bedroom. When I followed, some little time later, my feet were quiet on the stairs.

He was standing at the open wardrobe, running his hand along the silk of a black slip dress I'd bought from Ghost, eyes closed.

I touched my fingers to his back and that was all it took.

There was a scar, embossed like a lightning flash, across his chest; an-other, puckered like a closing rose, high on his thigh.

'Harry?'

Sweaty, the surprise still lingering in his eyes, he touched my breast with the tip of each of his fingers, the ball of his thumb.

After he'd gone, I bathed, changed the linen on the bed, saw to my face and hair and wondered how I would spend the rest of the day till, as promised, he returned. A little light shopping, lunch, perhaps an afternoon movie, a quiet stroll.

He was there at the door at eight o'clock sharp, freshly shaved, a clean shirt. Before kissing me he hesitated, as if I might have changed my mind, filed it away under Big Mistake. And when I kissed him back I could feel something shift within him, a deliverance from some small fear or doubt.

We made love and then we talked — I talked, in the main, and he listened. Marie had been right. Though as this night gradually became a second and a third and he felt more at ease, at home, he let slip bits and pieces of his life. How his wife had told him she was leaving him in an email because she was too scared to tell him face to face. That had been when he was on his second tour of Northern Ireland, in Belfast. She was living in Guildford now, remarried; he saw the two boys quite often, less often than he'd have liked. The eldest was away at university in Stirling, studying animal biology, the youngest was hoping to take up the law. Bright kids, he said, take after their mother. If either of them had gone into the army, she'd threatened to slit her wrists.

We started to fall into a routine: Fridays and Saturdays he would spend the evening, stay the night. If ever he came round in mid-week, he would go home and sleep in his own bed so as to make an early start. The ring from his finger had disappeared, to be replaced by a pale band of skin.

When finally I told him about Victor, the way he had made me feel, powerless, used, as if I had no will, no skin, there was something in his face I hadn't seen before. Something that made his body tense and his hands tighten into fists.

'People like that,' he said, 'they don't deserve to live.'

Victor sent me texts, left messages on my phone, to none of which I replied. He didn't like to be ignored. When finally he came round, it was not much after one in the morning, early for him. Possibly he'd been watching the house to see if Harry were there, I don't know. I opened the door part way and held it fast.

'What's the matter?' I said. 'Lost your way?'

'I wanted to see you.'

'All right, you have. Now you can go.'

He was wearing a new suit, expensive, six or seven hundred at least; his face still tanned from his time abroad, eyes small and dark and rarely still. The same old smile slipped into place with practised ease.

'It's been a long time,' he said.

'I hadn't noticed.'

'Liar.' His tongue showed for an instant, lizard-like, between thin lips.

'Good night, Victor.'

I leaned against the door to push it closed and he pushed back. Whether he meant it to or not, the edge of it caught me hard in the face, just alongside the eye, and I stumbled to my knees.

'Careful,' Victor said, shutting the door behind him. 'You could get hurt.'

He touched his finger to the well of blood and drew it down, slowly, across my cheek.

When he left, an hour later, all I could do was curl myself into a ball, cover my head and wish for sleep.

That was how Harry found me next morning, a surprise call on his way to work.

'This was Victor? He did this?'

Gingerly, I touched the side of my face. 'It was an accident, sort of an accident. I don't think it was meant.'

'Then how…?'

'Last night, he was here. I was trying to stop him from coming in.'

'He forced his way into the house, that's what you're saying?'

'Yes, I suppose so.'

'Suppose?'

'Well, yes, then. Yes.'

'And forced himself upon you?'

I turned my head away.

'He raped you.'

'No.'

'Then what else would you call it?'

I had begun to shake.

"I'll kill him, so help me, I will.'

'Harry, don't, please. Don't say that.'

'Just tell me where I can find him.'

'Harry, no.'

'You want this to happen again? Keep happening?'

'No, of course not.'

'Then tell me. And I'll put a stop to it, once and for all.'

I didn't tell him, not then. Not right away. The last thing I wanted was for him to go off angry and emotional, acting impulsively, without properly thinking it through. That he could kill a man, I had little doubt; he had killed men before, after all; men he didn't know, men at close range, men he couldn't — didn't — see. It was what he'd been trained to do. He could kill a man, I was sure, with his bare hands. Those hands.

'The Concord,' I said. 'You know, that place out towards the estuary. That's where he spends a lot of time. Victor. If you still did want to see him. Talk to him. He'd listen to you.'

It was the next evening, the two of us propped up on pillows after making love; Harry's head resting on my shoulder, my fingers combing through his hair.

'What if he doesn't?' Harry said.

'Hmm?'

'What if he doesn't listen?'

I reached down and kissed the palm of his hand. 'Maybe the club's not the best place to talk. Somewhere quieter might be better. Where he's less likely to make a fuss. The park, perhaps. Up river. Where they're filling in the old gravel pit. Somewhere like that.'

'He'd never come.'

'He might if he thought I was going to be there.'

I didn't say anything more about it; neither did he. Several more days passed. A week. Then…

'I'm meeting him this evening. Later. Where you said.'

'You're sure?'

His arms slid around me and I pressed my face against his chest.

'Don't trust him,' I said. 'Don't turn your back.'

I didn't see him again that night, nor for several nights after. I texted him to make sure he was all right and he was. 'Just busy. See you soon as I can.'

When he did come round I noticed some bruising, now fading, to the back of his hand; his knuckles were grazed. An accident, I thought, while working, a chisel that had slipped, a length of timber that had leaped back at his face.

'You saw him?'

'Yes, I saw him.'

He didn't tell me what had happened, what had been said. The only time I asked, weeks later, he said, 'You just don't want to know.'

Victor Sedalis had disappeared again, into thin air. Nobody asked questions or bothered to report him missing. After all, he'd done it before. Cyprus, this time, that was the story. Limassol, somewhere. Gambling debts he couldn't pay, the interest rising, compounding day by day.

'I shouldn't be surprised,' said the barman at the Concord, 'if this time he's gone for good.'

I continued to see a little of Harry, but after that it was never quite the same. The last I heard, he'd upped sticks and started a little boat-building business down near Southampton. One of his sons lives near there while he's studying for his doctorate. Biotechnology? Something like that?

At first there was the odd postcard or two, but Harry's not much of a one for writing and, I suppose, neither am I.

I did think about moving myself, got as far as putting the house on the market, but in the end I stayed. Too late to dig myself up, perhaps, too much effort transplanting myself, at this stage of my life. And, besides, I like it here. Where I know. It suits me. My little lunches with Marie. The tennis club. I can just about hold my end up at doubles, much to my surprise. And on a sunny day like today, I'll sometimes take a stroll down along the river to the country park. A few dog walkers, kids kicking a ball, quite often, weekdays, I've got the place to myself. Not that I mind. I feel safe there, secure. The ground fresh and firm beneath my feet.

My thanks to Amy Rigby and Bill Demain, whose song, 'Keep It To Yourself,' as sung by Amy, provided the initial idea for this story.

amyrigby.com

Ask Me Now

Tom Whitemore's father left him a set of golf clubs he had yet to use, a collection of the maritime novels of Patrick O'Brian, and an abiding love of Louis Armstrong and Duke Ellington.

Few visits to the retirement chalet in Devon where the older man lived out his last days were allowed to pass without his father reminiscing about the time he had seen Louis on a revolving stage at the Empress Hall, his warm-up act a one-legged tap dancer called Peg Leg Bates; or the Ellington concert when the young English tenor player, Tubby Hayes, had walked on stage, mid-number, and, to the audience's amazed recognition, taken the vacant seat in otherwise all-American all-star saxophone section.

No matter how many times told, Whitemore listened to the stories with pleasure, sharing, for a few vicarious moments, his father's surge of patriotism as he relived the latter, the tear that wavered in the corner of an eye. Try as he might, he could never quite bring himself to believe in the one-legged dancer.

Louis, though… when his father had suffered his third and fatal heart attack, Armstrong's trumpet had been peeling out a succession of high Cs in the final chorus of "Hotter Than That", each one clear as a bell; the album still slowly revolving on the turntable when the carer had found his father's body wedged between his wheelchair and a chest of drawers, the stylus trapped in the run-off groove, fast against the label.

In contrast, all Whitemore's wife had left him, the day she drove off to her parents in Chapel St. Leonard's, taking the twins, was a note propped against the burned-out toaster in the kitchen.

I'm sorry, Tom, I can't take it any more. I just can't…

That had been six years ago.

His father had been dead for ten.

Whitemore was still in the same house, a lodger upstairs in the twins' room Monday to Friday, and he was still doing the same job — the one his wife had hated — detective sergeant in the Public Protection Team: domestic violence, hate crime, serious sexual abuse, assault.

Scum, Tom, that's what they are. Who you spend your days and nights with. Scum of the earth, and then you bring them home to us.

She turned aside from his face, flinched at his touch. Flinched when he held one or other of the twins in his arms, helped them to undress, softly kissed the tops of their heads, ran the flannel across them in the bath.

I'm sorry, Tom…

For a while, the first year or so if not more, he had allowed himself to think it was temporary, a break to clear the air; sooner or later things would even out, Marianne would come to her senses, move back home with the children. His children. She couldn't stay with her parents for ever, after all.

So Whitemore drove out to see them every other weekend without fail: spent time with the boys, a game of soccer on the beach then late Sunday lunch around the table, Yorkshire pudding, roast potatoes, gravy. Barely a voice raised over whatever music was playing, subdued, in the next room. The twins keeping their eyes on their plates, snatching an occasional glance at dad or mum.

'Boys,' Marianne's mother said abruptly one afternoon, when he was in the kitchen, helping with the washing up. 'Young boys especially. More than anything they need a father.' Smiling faintly, she handed him a dry tea towel. 'That's what I think, at least. Not that anyone's asked.'

Encouraged, Whitemore smiled back.

He hadn't quite understood.

Marianne followed him out to the car and suggested they take a walk before he left. It was coming on dark, the wind relenting off the sea. Faint in the distance, the lights of Skegness.

Tom, I've met someone…

Bile rose high in his throat and stuck.

All he remembered of the divorce was signing papers, feeling numb. They were going to live in Lincoln, Marianne, the children and the new husband, close by the cathedral, a new home, ready and waiting. When he got to see the twins now it was more awkward, less often; listless afternoons in Burger King straining for something to say. Biting his tongue while the boys flicked ketchup-coated fries at one another when they thought he wasn't looking, kicking each other beneath the table, harder and harder until he finally snapped.

He'd not long returned from one such visit, the afternoon ending in sour looks and recrimination, when the phone shook him out of his misery. Heather Jeffries, the senior social worker attached to the team, low-voiced, level-headed.

'Tom, hoped I might catch you. The meeting in the morning — any chance of a coffee beforehand?'

There was a café off the Old Market Square — in truth, there were several, this one quieter, less fashionable. Formica tables. Posters of old Italian movies on the wall. Whitemore thought he recognised Gina Lollobrigida, Sophia Loren.

The choice of coffees was simple: large or small, white or black. He placed his order, picked up the cups from the counter and carried them across.

Heather dropped two tiny sweeteners into hers and stirred. 'Emma Laurie, Tom, ring any bells…?'

Whitemore pictured a wraith-like woman with wispy hair, cigarette burns on her arms. Late twenties, looking older. For a time she'd lived with a man he'd been supervising, an ex-offender: it had not gone well.

'Three kids, wasn't it?' Whitemore said. 'All taken into care. Rory, Jason and… I don't remember the girl… Julie, maybe?'

'Jade. The boys are both fostered out now — together by some small miracle and happy as Larry. Jade's been back home with her mum the best part of a year. A few wobbles, but until recently it's seemed to be just about okay.'

'And now?'

'Helen Bailey, she's the family's social worker…'

'I know Helen.'

'Three times she's been round in the last few weeks wanting to see Jade and each time there's been some excuse. Sorry, but Jade's on a sleepover with a friend; Jade's been up all night with a poorly tummy, throwing up and everything, and now she's upstairs sleeping — could Helen not come back another time rather than wake her? When she went back the next day as arranged, there was nobody there. Phoned that evening to see what had happened, the bloke Emma's been seeing had borrowed his mate's van and taken them off to Mablethorpe for the day. Surprise treat.'

'And Helen, she thinks there's more to it?'

'Wouldn't you?'

'Likely.'

'Last thing she wants, Helen, a situation where she keeps getting fobbed off till it's too late. For the girl's sake as well as her own. Jade ends up in hospital or worse and it's Helen's name that's splashed all over the paper. Another social worker falling down on the job. The media only too anxious to hang her out to dry. Neglect and worse. People baying for her blood.'

'You really think it's that serious? For Jade, I mean.'

'That's it, I just don't know. Helen could be being over-cautious, reading the signs wrongly...' Jeffries sighed, pushed her cup aside. 'There's another thing. Emma's pregnant again. Three months since. I thought she might opt for a termination, but no. Left to herself, maybe she would have, and maybe for the best. But this man, the new boyfriend...'

'He's the father?'

Jeffries nodded. 'Wheelan. Garry Wheelan. Two Rs. Won't hear of it. Like it was his decision, not hers.'

'And what? Another child, a baby, you're afraid she won't cope?'

'I don't think she'll find it easy. If there is something going on with Jade, especially.'

'And this Wheelan... ?'

'Ex-army. Local.'

'Anything known? Cause for concern?'

'Ran the DBS checks, naturally. Three arrests in as many years. Two for common assault, one for criminal damage. Never charged.'

'This was before he got together with Emma or after?'

'Before.'

'And he was in the army how long?'

'Ten years, give or take.'

'Afghanistan?'

'Yes. Iraq before that.'

Whitemore looked to where the inside of the window was beaded with condensation. 'It takes time to settle back into normal life, you know that as well as anyone. Perhaps this was what he needed. Chance to settle down.'

'I'd like to think so.'

'But you don't.'

'I'm worried, Tom, that's all. Emma and Jade, it's been touch and go like I say. Come close once or twice to Jade going back into care. And Emma, as we know, she's not been brilliant at coping. Add a baby, an ex-squaddie with a temper; a proclivity, maybe, for violence. All together in that little two up, two down.'

'This will all come up at the meeting.'

'I know, but…'

'But you thought I might ask around, circumstances of those arrests. Put a little flesh on the bones. Have a word with him later, perhaps? If it seems appropriate. Garry with two Rs.'

Heather Jeffries smiled. 'You'll keep Helen in the loop?'

'Of course.'

She glanced at her watch. 'Best get our skates on. Don't want them starting without us.'

Two days later, when Whitemore finally made it home after a more-than-twelve-hour shift, head throbbing and only a week-old ready meal from Sainsbury's between himself and what felt like near-starvation, the missed call light on his phone was glowing.

'Tom, hi. It's Helen. I tried your mobile earlier. Give me a call if you get a chance, okay?

He listened to the message again before pressing erase; fished a packet of Ibuprofen from the kitchen drawer, set the kettle to boil and dropped a teabag into the Forest mug one of the twins, Adam, had bought him for Christmas. Ignoring the date on the Thai chicken curry, he placed it in the microwave and flicked the switch.

A considerable part of his morning had been spent with a seventeen-year-old rape victim, who had decided, after being harassed on Twitter, Facebook and Instagram, to withdraw the complaint against her attacker. After which, together with a member of the probation service and a social worker, he'd sat round a table at the Hockley office of Recovery in Nottingham, determining which of the available programmes would be most suitable for a twenty-two-year-old who'd gone into prison clean and been released with a serious drug problem eighteen months later.

He tipped the food out on to a plate and unfolded that day's copy of the *Post*. Plans to extend the city's tram network were set to go ahead. A mass brawl outside a takeaway in Aspley had resulted in three men being taken to Queen's Medical Centre with serious injuries. After picking at the curry a while longer he forked the remainder into the bin.

'Helen? Hi, it's Tom. Just got your message.'

Sometimes callers on the landline seemed oddly distant, their voices blurred across several timelines; Helen Bailey's was so clear she could have been in the next room.

'Garry Wheelan, you haven't a chance… ?'

'No, I'm sorry.'

'No problem. I know you're busy. It's just I went round there, Emma's, this afternoon. Caught a glimpse of Jade in the other room before they could scoot her away. Plaster to one side of her head, what looked like bruising. She fell, Garry said when I asked…'

'Garry said… ?'

'Yes. Racing round the back ginnel like a silly thing, he said, went sprawling. I asked did they take her to A & E in case, you know, there was a concussion, but no, he said, why all that fuss? Emma washed it clean, stuck on a plaster and kissed it better.'

'And Jade?'

'She seemed all right, I suppose. Not easy to tell.'

'Kids fall over,' Whitemore said. 'It's what they do. Happens all the time.'

It hung in the air between them, buoyed up by the faint sound of her breathing.

'I'll get on to it,' Whitemore said. 'First thing.'

He was halfway through dialling his ex-wife's number, over a week since he'd spoken to the twins, when he reconsidered — if they hadn't turned in already there would be some barbed remark from Marianne about getting them all excited just before bedtime.

Twenty minutes of the news and he was ready for bed himself, knowing that once there he'd find it nigh-impossible to fall asleep. How wrong could he be? Next he knew it was 4.30 in the morning and he needed to pee.

The street was short and narrow, the houses squat and, here and there, in sore need of care. Emma Laurie's lay towards the far end, where the terrace halted abruptly at a patch of barren ground. Mismatching curtains were closed across the windows, shutting out the meagre light.

Stepping up to the door, Whitemore's mind was hauled back seven years: the death of Emma's previous partner at his own hand, a Stanley knife resting on the bath edge alongside a pale oval of soap. In a ramshackle shed in the back yard, children's faces staring up at him from the cloistered dark.

'You! What the fuck you doin' here?'

'Hello, Emma.'

Hair pulled harshly back from her face, tiredness darkening her eyes, she was wearing grey sweat pants and a matching hoodie, the baby just starting to show.

'I was close by,' Whitemore said. 'Thought I'd stop off and see how you were.'

'Lyin' bastard.' Said with the hint of a smile.

He followed her inside, through a room where clothes hung drying before one bar of an electric fire and into a kitchen with a folding table pushed to one side, plates and bowls in the sink waiting to be washed; the faint smell of toast.

Emma rinsed out a couple of mugs, took a carton of milk from the fridge. There was an ultrasound image fixed to the fridge door.

'How's it going?' Whitemore asked. 'The baby?'

71

She shrugged.

'Boy or girl?'

'Not gonna matter, is it?'

'How d'you mean?'

'Your lot, soon as I've dropped it, fallin' over backwards for the chance to take it away.'

'Come on, Emma, that's not true.'

'No? Why's that skinny bitch round here all the time then, sticking her nose in?'

'Helen, you mean?'

'Always questions. Questions, questions, questions. Jade, how's she eatin', is she putting on weight, how's she gettin' on at school? Like it was her business. How'd she get that bruise? Cut the size of my little fingernail and it's did we take her to doctor, take her up to A & E…'

'She's concerned.'

'Concerned, all right. Bending her scrawny arse over backwards, lookin' for a reason to hoik Jade back into care. Baby too, when it comes.'

'Emma, I don't think it's like that at all.'

'No? Well, you would say that, wouldn't you? Sugar in this or not?'

Emma moved the washing away from the fire and switched on the extra bar. They sat either side of the flat screen TV, framed photos of Jade and her two brothers on the narrow ledge above the fireplace; Jade smiling uncertainly towards the camera, a stray length of hair falling across her face; both lads secondary school age by now, straight and proud in their uniforms — What had Emma Jeffries said? Happy as Larry? — new family, new lives. They would be, Whitemore thought, around the same age as his own.

'Do you see much of them?' he asked. 'The boys?'

'Christmas. Birthdays. Might bump into 'em once in a while, you know, round town.' She shook her head. 'Garry wanted to take 'em to City Ground one time. You'd've thought he wanted to cart 'em off other side of the bloody world.'

'I was hoping Garry might be around.'

'How's that, then?'

'Just a chat.'

'Not in any trouble, is he?'

'Not as far as I know.'

'Sorted himself out, has Garry. Since he's been with me. Quietened down.'

'That's good to hear.'

'Still gets these headaches, mind. Trouble sleeping. But he's quit the drinking. Bar a pint or two, weekends.' She lit a cigarette from the fire. 'Quiet, too. Too much so for my liking, sometimes. Sits where you are, staring off into space, God knows where he really is, but wherever it is it's not here. Back there somewhere, I suppose. Some godforsaken place or other.'

Whitemore nodded, sipped his tea. The sound of someone's television was leaking through from next door, the bass beat of a car stereo parked close by.

'You don't know when he might be back?'

Emma shook her head. 'Once he's out, he's out all day. Till Jade gets home at least. You could try the library, Angel Row. Sits in there sometimes and reads. Or the Arboretum. Wanders round there, the rose garden, says it clears his head.'

There was no sign of Garry Wheelan in the library. By the time Whitemore reached the Arboretum, cutting down past the southern edge of the cemetery, a faint rain had begun to fall. Wheelan was sitting on one of the benches surrounding the Chinese Bell pagoda, close by the cannons brought back in triumph from the Crimean War. Green waterproof jacket, boots, jeans; lean face, pale eyes, dark hair clipped short.

He scarcely looked up as Whitemore approached.

Said nothing as he sat down.

'I'm...' Whitemore began.

'I know who you are. Emma texted me, said you'd likely be nosing round.'

'I just wanted...'

'To have a chat, she said. Didn't say what about.'

'Cases like Emma's...'

73

'That was she is? A case?'

'Situations like Emma's, where there's been some concern in the past about the children in her care. We have to think about the appropriateness of any close relationships she may have formed...'

'That nonce, Darren?'

'Yes, Darren...'

'Pathetic bastard.'

'Maybe.' The bathroom door had been bolted from the inside; one of his arms had hung down inside the bath, the other trailed towards the floor.

'You're not saying I'm like him? That prick. Cause if you are...' Wheelan facing him now, one of his boots starting to beat a slow tattoo on the ground.

Whitemore held his gaze, waiting for him to relax.

'That bother you got yourself into a while back, I've been talking to the officers concerned. From what I can tell, it was mostly a case of you getting drawn into something not of your making. The last time, for instance...'

'Ignorant bastard, mouthing off about the army. Got what he was asking for.'

'Got you into trouble.'

'It was worth it.'

'You think so?'

Wheelan shook his head. 'It's different now.'

Close to where they were sitting a blackbird was busily arguing a worm from the soil.

'You want to walk for a bit?' Whitemore said.

They went up past the pagoda towards the Addison Street entrance and turned right along the road that would take them down by the university buildings and into the city centre.

'Emma mentioned you'd been having trouble sleeping.'

No reply. The rain a little heavier now. Wheelan staring straight ahead.

'Bad dreams, maybe? Headaches that won't go away?'

'Know it all, don't you?'

'Bits and pieces. Men I've had some contact with in the past. Odd things I've read.'

Wheelan laughed derisively. 'Things you've fucking read!'

They came to halt at the junction with Shakespeare Street, the Orange Tree pub in front of them, the old library at their backs.

'You know there's help available, people you can speak to...'

'Yeah. Sit round and — what was it? — explore your emotions and trauma in the company of fellow sufferers. Well, bollocks to that. What I want to do is shut that crap out of my mind once and for all, not bring it all back so's some psychiatrist can wet himself. Write a fucking book about it.'

He was several strides away when Whitemore called him back.

'Being a father to Emma's baby. Being responsible. How d'you feel about that?'

'You got kids?'

'Yes. Two.'

'Then how d'you think I feel? Ask your fucking self.'

The next day began with Whitemore doing his best to reassure the mother of a vulnerable sixteen-year-old in custody that every effort would be made to ensure he did no further self-harm, and ended with a lengthy meeting at which Ben Leonard, the community psychiatric nurse attached to the unit, introduced a new set of proposals for safely re-integrating offenders with mental health issues back into the community.

It was past eight and dark by the time he got home; the rain that had started earlier that day still falling. There was a heavy-looking bundle on the path beside the front door.

As Whitemore drew closer the bundle moved and raised its head. It was Adam.

Whitemore eased him inside, stripped off his sodden coat, towelled his hair, chafed warmth back into his hands. Careful, so far, to avoid asking what he was doing there, all the other questions busy in his mind.

Fifteen or so minutes later, Adam dwarfed inside one of his father's jumpers, central heating turned up to full, they were sitting across from one another, mugs of hot chocolate in their hands.

Looking at him, trying not to stare at the tousled hair, the almost-violet skin around the boy's downturned eyes, Whitemore felt something inside him lurch. Love, for want of a better name.

'Do they know you're here?'

'Who?'

'Mum and… and Colin.'

'Course not.'

'I'll have to phone them.'

'No.'

'Adam, I must. They'll be worried sick.'

'Not now. Not yet.'

'I have to.'

There were three missed calls on his mobile; texts he hadn't read; after switching his phone off for the meeting he'd forgotten to switch it back on.

Marianne picked up at the first ring.

'Adam, is he…?'

'He's here.'

'Thank God.'

Behind Marianne's relieved sobs, Whitemore could hear a man's voice, urgent and questioning.

'I'd only just got back,' Whitemore said, 'and he was here waiting.'

'How on earth did he get all that way?'

'By train.'

'But how… ?'

'Money he got for Christmas, that's what he said.'

'And he's all right?'

'He's fine.'

The same voice again in the background — Colin's, he assumed — raised in exasperation. 'All right, all right,' he heard Marianne saying. 'But just wait, please.'

'Fine!' and a door slamming.

The click of a glass and then the sound of his wife — his ex-wife — lighting a cigarette, exhaling.

'He told his brother,' Marianne said, 'he was going to a friend's house to play some game or other. Colin went round to collect him. That was the first we knew.'

'He says Colin hit him.'

'What?'

76

'Adam. He says Colin hit him. That's why he ran away.'

'It was nothing.'

'Really?'

'Just some silly argument over nothing at all.'

'His phone. That's what it was about. That's what he says.'

'He wouldn't stop fiddling with it, all through dinner. No matter how many times he was told not to.'

'And when he didn't stop Colin hit him.'

'No.'

'He didn't hit him, is that what you're saying?'

'Not because of that.'

'Then why?'

'Colin took the phone away from him, tried to, and Adam told him to fuck off.'

'And that's when he hit him?'

'He lost his temper. It happens.'

'How often?'

'Sorry?'

'How often does he lose his temper?'

'He doesn't.'

'No? Adam says he slapped him round the back of the head so hard it knocked him out of his chair. Or is that an exaggeration?'

'No.' Quietly. 'No, it's not.'

There were things Whitemore wanted to say best left to another day.

'I'll drive him back over in the morning.'

'Thank you.'

Whitemore broke the connection.

The sky had cleared into a conglomeration of muted blues and greys, the spire of the cathedral rising into view when they were still some way distant. Whitemore had pressed play on the car stereo as they were approaching Newark, shuffled through Ellington at Newport, Basie, Louis Armstrong at the Crescendo, but none had suited his mood.

Adam had barely spoken for most of the journey, sitting hunched in the passenger seat, barely moving save occasionally to shift his balance, check his phone. At breakfast he had asked, not looking up as he did so, why did he have to stay living in Lincoln, why couldn't he move back to Nottingham, live there with him?

'It's not that straightforward,' Whitemore said.

'Why not? I'm here, aren't I?' Adam looking at him now. 'You don't have to take me back at all. Not today. They can just send my clothes, right? Anything else I need. And I'll get to change schools. Somewhere where I won't be being picked on all the time.'

'Is that what happens?'

Adam pushed how bowl away. 'Why can't I do that? Why? Go on, just tell me why.'

'Look, Adam, you're only saying all this because you're still angry and upset.'

'I'm not.'

'I think you are. And besides, imagine what it'd be like. You'd scarcely know anyone for one thing, wouldn't have any friends…'

'I could make new friends.'

'You'd miss Matthew… and your mum.'

'Yeah, well, least I wouldn't be living with him. Bloody Colin.'

Whitemore sighed, looked at his watch. 'We ought to be making a move.'

On the way out to the car Adam caught hold of his sleeve. 'Dad. Seriously. Why can't I? Move back here, I mean.'

'It wasn't what we agreed.'

'Who? Who agreed? Not me.'

'Me and your mum.'

'That's not fair.'

'I know.'

Whitemore reached out to touch his son's hair, but the boy swerved smartly away.

As soon as the front door opened, Adam scuttled in under his mother's gaze and scurried upstairs, leaving Whitemore not knowing whether to kiss Marianne briefly on the cheek or stand there smiling half-heartedly and wait.

'Well,' she said, 'You'd better come in.'

The kitchen was at the back of the house, looking out over the garden; an extension, partly covered in glass.

'Coffee, Tom?'

'No, it's okay.'

'It's no problem.'

'All right, then. Thanks.'

When he saw her now, it was impossible to understand what there had ever been between them.

'How is he?' Marianne asked. 'Adam?'

'Hurt. Angry. He says he wants to move out, come and live with me.'

'Of course he does.'

'Why of course?'

'He was too young to remember what it was like.'

Whitemore gazed out into the garden: neat clumps of shrubs, compost, a football, in one corner a camellia coming into bloom.

'Colin's not here then?'

'No. He had to go to work. A meeting…'

'Some client with wealth management problems, I don't doubt.'

'Tom, don't start…'

'Bespoke financial plan in need a bit of buffering.'

'Christ, Tom!'

'What?'

'You know how… how petty you sound? How bloody self-righteous?'

'Well, whatever he's doing, he's not here is he, that's the point. And he's not here because he hasn't got the guts, after what he's done, to see me face to face.'

'What were you going to do, then, Tom? Punch him one? Arrest him?'

'Maybe both.'

'God, you really are pathetic.'

'Yes, well, we know that, don't we? And what you were ever doing, wasting five years of your precious life with me, we'll never fucking know!'

Marianne pulled both hands deliberately away from the tray she was carrying, letting coffee pot, jug, cups and saucers crash to the floor.

'Stop it!' Adam screamed from the doorway, face distorting. 'Stop it, why don't you? Just stop!'

A change in the weather, is that really all it took? Mornings when the air was crisp, the light clear and more shades of blue in the sky than you could ever hope to identify.

Whitemore dug out an old pair of trainers from the bottom of the wardrobe and started going for a morning run. Marianne, relenting, trying to rebuild bridges, said if he had any leave owing, why didn't he take the twins away for a few days during their Easter break? Whitemore booked them into a B & B in Whitby, up on the North Yorks coast, visited the abbey, played football on the beach, tramped across the cliffs to Robin Hood's Bay and sat high above the tide line eating fish and chips. Enjoying an after work drink with Helen Bailey one evening, she told him any worries she'd had about Jade were almost certainly unfounded; Emma's pregnancy was progressing pretty much as normal, and if Emma hadn't stopped smoking entirely, at least she'd cut back to one or two a day. Ben Leonard had contrived to bump into Garry Wheelan in Angel Row Library and convinced him that talking to one of the doctors at the Priory about his recurring headaches and insomnia might not be a total waste of time.

Too good to last?

Whitemore was relaxing at home, the end of a not-too-stressful day, a small glass of whisky by his side, Glenmorangie, single malt; one of his father's old albums on the turntable — Armstrong, the Hot Sevens — when the phone called him back across the room. A domestic, Forest Fields, one of his.

By the time he arrived there were two police cars and an ambulance, beat officers doing their best to keep a conglomeration of gawkers at bay.

The front room was a disaster: the kitchen little better. Sticks of broken furniture, curtains torn down and ripped across, shredded cushions, shattered plates and mugs; the television set lay in the centre of the floor, screen splintered across. Only the framed photographs of Jade and her brothers seemed to have survived unscathed, perched precariously on the shelf above the fireplace, looking on.

Jade herself was in the back of the ambulance, being treated by one of the paramedics for a cut on her forehead, where she had been struck by flying glass.

Emma was sitting on the stairs, heavily pregnant, half-dazed, a cigarette burning away between her fingers, all but forgotten. After talking to the officers who had responded to the call, Whitemore squeezed himself onto the stairs beside her; took the smouldering cigarette from her hand and stubbed it out on the sole of his shoe.

'What happened?'

He had to ask several times before she replied.

'I dunno, he just… he just went mad, really mad, lost it, lost it altogether.'

'Garry?'

'Garry. Screaming an' shoutin'. Throwing things. Smashing furniture. Everything. Took hold o'me, didn't he? Lifted me up in the air… I thought, I dunno what I thought… pissin' meself, I don't mind tellin' you. Thought he was gonna say somethin' but he never did. Just sort of stared then put me back down, careful, careful as you like. Walked out. Jade was cryin', blood runnin' down her face and cryin'. Cryin' for him to come back. Mad bastard, he never did. I hope he never does.'

'What started it?' Whitemore asked. 'Kicked it all off?'

Emma shook her head.

'We was just sittin' there, normal like, you know? I'd not long made us a cup of tea. Some rubbish on the telly. Garry, he was quiet, yeah, but no quieter'n usual. I s'pose I might have been talking 'bout the baby. Talking too much, maybe. Silly stuff, really. Then it kicked, really hard, you know, the baby, and I said somethin' like, here Garry, feel that, an' took hold if his hand and put it there — here — like I'd done before, plenty of times, but this time…'

Whitemore thought she was about to cry, but instead she looked down at her empty hand.

'Don't s'pose you've got a cigarette, have you?'

A sliver of moon slipped out from behind a cloud then disappeared: the sky over the city never really dark, a persistent orange glow.

Whitemore could just distinguish the shape, hunched forward, face lost in shadow. The same bench as before.

Wheelan scarcely looked up as Whitemore approached, sat down. 'How is she? Emma?'

'Pretty much as you'd expect. Uncomprehending. Frightened.'

'And the girl?'

'Bar a couple of stitches, she'll be okay.'

'Thank Christ.'

'It could've been worse.'

'Think I don't know that?'

Something scuttled along the hedgerow at their backs. Whitemore conscious of the other man's breathing, his proximity, the sudden movement of his foot as it scraped against gravel and then was still.

Minutes passed. More.

Voices, sudden and raucous, from the far side of the park.

The occasional car passing along Waverley Street towards the Forest.

'Helmand,' Wheelan said suddenly. 'We were in Helmand. Nahr-e Saraj. Lost someone there to snipers the day before. Out on patrol. Three days before it had been an IED. Two seriously wounded, one trapped inside. It was a bad time.

'We'd had intelligence of Taliban holed up in a building that had been a school. Before the Taliban shut it down. Went in at night. Not like this. Real night. Stars and fuck all else. Best chance of taking the bastards by surprise.

'I was in the lead group, two in front, Preston and Jagger, me and McQuaid close behind. Couple of stun grenades and then we're in, hollering at the tops of our voices, all bloody hell breaking loose, automatic fire from the top of the stairs. "Left, left!" McQuaid shouts, pointing, and I'm ducking low, pushing through into this room, and as soon as I'm inside there's movement along the side wall, hands raised as if holding a weapon, and I'm firing, two bursts and then a third to be sure, over before it's begun, and then there's a light over my shoulder and I can see what I've done.

'The boy was maybe eight or nine, no older, a good half of his face gone missing. The girl was younger, four or five at most, some kind of doll clutched fast against her nightshirt with both hands. Except it wasn't a doll.

"'Jesus fuck!" McQuaid said over my shoulder. "Get the fuck out of here now."

'Searched the place from top to bottom. No hidden weapons and if the Taliban had been there, they were on their toes before we arrived. Before heading back to camp, we called in an air strike, razed the place to the ground.'

When Whitemore shivered he tried to tell himself it was the cold.

'That's what you see?' he said. 'In your dreams?'

'In my dreams they're still alive, still breathing. Holding out their hands towards me, speaking in a language I don't understand. If I help them I can stop them dying. The girl, she looks a bit like Jade, but younger.'

He got to his feet.

'Some time when Emma's not around, I'll get my stuff.'

'You sure?'

'What was it you said before? The appropriateness of any relationships she may have formed? I think we both know the answer to that.'

Whitemore watched him walk away, head down, dissolving into the pattern of the surrounding trees.

Emma's baby was born at four in the morning after a prolonged labour, a dark-haired, dark-eyed girl weighing six pounds, nine ounces. Jade was delighted with her new baby sister, Emma exhausted. Whitemore let Garry Wheelan know as promised, and three days after mother and baby returned home, a parcel arrived with a West Midlands postmark, a rag doll with a pink dress and ribbons in her hair wrapped in tissue paper, and a card offering congratulations. Unsigned.

'This'll be from your dad,' Emma said, 'More than likely.' And she lay the doll carefully down alongside the baby.

Dead Dames Don't Sing

Once upon a time Jack Kiley lived over a bookshop in Belsize Park. Nights he couldn't sleep, and there were many, he'd soft-foot downstairs and browse the shelves. Just like having his own private library. Patrick Hamilton, he was a particular favourite for a while, perversity in the seedier backstreets of pre-war London: *The Siege of Pleasure*, *Hangover Square*. Then it was early Graham Greene, Eric Ambler, Gerald Kersh. He was four chapters into *Night and the City* when the envelope, pale blue and embossed across the seal, was slipped beneath his door. Notice to quit. The shop was being taken over by a larger concern and there were alternative plans for the building's upper floors that didn't include having a late-fortyish private detective, ex-Metropolitan police, as tenant. Kiley scoured the pages of the local press, skimmed the internet, made a few calls: the result, two rooms plus a bathroom and minuscule kitchen above a charity shop in a less buoyant part of north London, namely Tufnell Park. If not exactly low rent, it was at least affordable. Just. And no more a true park than its upscale neighbour.

Having to pass through the shop on his way upstairs, Kiley's eye grew used to picking out the occasional bargain newly arrived on the rail: a v-necked sweater from French Connection, forty percent cashmere; a pair of black denim jeans, by the look of them barely worn, and fortuitously his size, 36" waist, 32" inside leg. The book section was seldom to his taste, too many discarded copies of J.K. Rowling and *Fifty Shades of Grey*, whereas the ever-changing box of CDs offered up the more-than-occasional gem. A little soul, late 50s Sinatra, Merle Haggard, a little jazz. He was listening to *Blues With a Reason*, Chet Baker, when his mobile intervened.

'Jack? I'm across the street at Bear and Wolf if you'd care to join me.'

Kiley pressed stop on the stereo and reached for his shoes.

Bear and Wolf was an upscale coffee shop with more than half an eye on the growing number of affluent couples and laptop-toting singles newly moved into the area, the women unstylishly stylish in a cool kind of way, the men mostly tall and bulky and distinguished by their lumberjack shirts and metrosexual beards.

Kiley made his way past the workaholics hot-desking at the front table and, pausing at the counter just long enough to order a flat white, ran the gauntlet of buggies and small children to where Kate Keenan was sitting, an oasis of apparent calm around her, in the furthest corner. Kate looked unimpeachable in a dark linen trouser suit and cream shirt, dark hair framing her face as she smiled.

'So, Jack. Long time, no see.'

It had been a month or so back, a Private View for an exhibition of Saul Leiter photographs at The Photographers' Gallery, Kate there to do a piece for *The Independent*, one of the last before the print edition of the paper folded. Kiley had liked the photos, the colour shots especially, but felt uneasy in the crowd. After twenty minutes he'd made his excuses and left.

'Been keeping busy, I trust?' Kate asked now.

'Not so you'd notice.'

'Don't tell me things in the PI business are slowing down?'

Kiley shrugged. Kate liked to tease him in a good-natured way about his late-chosen profession, referring to it with appropriate hard-boiled inflections, as if he were some combination of Sam Spade and Philip Marlowe, instead of an ex-copper who'd once played soccer in the lower leagues and now spent his time investigating dodgy insurance claims, snooping on behalf of a local firm of solicitors or shadowing errant wives.

'Only, if you're not overburdened, there might be something I could pass your way.'

'And here was I thinking this wasn't going to be business but pleasure.'

'Can't it be both?'

'Not recently.'

An eyebrow was raised. 'You shouldn't keep walking out on me so early.'

'It's not you, it's just…'

'The company I keep? Too arty, too cerebral for a down-to-earth guy like you?'

'Too up themselves, don't forget that.'

Kate laughed. 'Jack, you're so full of shit.'

'Difference is, I know it.'

Whatever response Kate had lined up was halted by the arrival of Kiley's flat white, the shape of a left-leaning heart traced through the crema on the surface.

'Why do we argue all the time, Jack?' Kate asked, after Kiley had taken his first approving taste.

'It stops us jumping all over one another?'

Leaning forward, she brushed her fingers across the back of his hand. 'In that case, couldn't we agree not to argue for the next hour or so?'

Kiley was looking quizzically at his watch. 'You do realise it's eleven-forty in the morning?'

'You could always drink that slowly. Then it'll be afternoon.'

When Jack awoke Kate was lying with one leg stretched across the back of his, the other angled up towards her chest. Supple for a woman gradually edging closer to fifty than forty, Jack thought. All that yoga, he supposed. Pilates. In the half-light that filtered through the blinds, the skin at the curve of her shoulder shone with a roseate glow.

Kiley's bladder insisted he slide himself free, and when he returned Kate was sitting up against the pillows, legs crossed at the ankles, elbows resting on her knees.

'Tea?' Kiley said.

'Tea.'

'Builders' okay?'

'Builders' is fine.'

While the kettle was boiling, he set the Chet Baker back on but, seeing Kate's frown, changed it for some Chopin nocturnes he'd brought up from downstairs on a whim and not yet played.

'Is your shower working?' Kate asked.

'Last time I tried.'

Clean, refreshed, she pulled on one of his T-shirts, a white towel wrapped around her head, and took her tea into the room that served as both living room and office.

'So are you going to tell me now?' Kiley asked. 'This proposition you mentioned?'

'You mean now we've got the preliminaries out of the way?'

'Exactly.'

'Very well. I've a friend who owns a specialist book store. Deals in first editions, original manuscripts, authors' letters, anything literary that's collectable and hard to find.'

Pausing, she sipped her tea.

'He's been offered something which, if it's kosher, might turn out to be a significant find. At the asking price, even something of a bargain.'

'And the problem?'

'He's been in the business long enough not to trust bargains.'

'What sort of money are we talking here, this manuscript, whatever it is?'

'Well, top end, a draft of a Sherlock Holmes short story in Conan Doyle's own hand just fetched upwards of $400,000 at auction in New York. Count down from there. But not too far.'

Kiley pursed his lips.

'This friend…'

'Daniel. Daniel Pike. Most of the serious dealers are in Cecil Court, but, for reasons best known to himself, his shop is in Camden Passage. He's expecting you this afternoon between three and four. And don't worry, friend or no friend, it's not pro bono; he'll pay usual rates at least.'

Ever since Kate had cajoled him into accompanying her to a screening of *The Big Sleep*, part of a Howard Hawks season at the South Bank, Kiley had entertained the fantasy that all rare book stores were staffed by attractive women with more than a passing resemblance to a young Dorothy Malone. Women who, given some small encouragement, would remove their spectacles, shake down their hair and set the sign on the door to closed.

Not so.

If anything, Daniel Pike bore a passing resemblance to Sidney Greenstreet, but a Greenstreet significantly slimmed down and confined to a wheelchair, white hair straying either side of a jowly face. Propelling himself around from behind his desk, he shook Kiley's hand firmly enough, then gestured for him to take a seat.

'I don't know how much Kate has explained,' Pike said in a gravelly voice.

'Beyond the fact that someone's offered to sell you what you consider to be a dodgy proposition, next to nothing at all.'

'Very well.' Pike eased himself back behind his crowded desk. 'How are you on poetry, Jack? Mid-twentieth century, British.'

'Questions like that in the pub quiz, I make my excuses and go for a slash.'

'So, William Pierce, that name doesn't mean anything?'

Kiley shook his head.

'Hughes, Larkin, Seamus Heaney, they're the ones most strongly recognised, all dead and gone now, of course. But behind those, Championship, if you like, instead of Premier League, there's a whole batch of others. Also, mostly passed on. Peter Redgrove. R.S. Thomas. William Pierce. More. Of those, partly because his output was, shall we say, shaky — small collections in even smaller editions — it's Pierce who's become the most collectable in recent years and whose reputation has risen accordingly.'

'And it's one of those small editions you're wary of buying?'

'Not exactly.' Pike changed position in his chair. 'What I've been offered is not a volume of poetry, but the manuscript of a novel. A crime novel it's claimed Pierce wrote when he was a young man as a means of making money, but which was never published.'

'Never published why?'

'I can't be certain, but it's possible he simply changed his mind. He was just beginning to gain some critical recognition and this novel, from what I've so far seen — fifty or so pages of typescript — well, let's say it wouldn't exactly have endeared him to the literary establishment.'

'Crime novels not ranking high in their estimation.'

'That depends. It's more the kind of crime novel he opted for. Something along the lines of Christie, Dorothy L. Sayers — the cosy kind where the butler did it with the candlestick in the library — that would have been acceptable. But this seems to be aiming at the more sensational end of the market. Pulp fiction in the style of someone like James Hadley Chase or Peter Cheyney.' Pike smiled. 'Hard, fast and deadly.'

Kiley nodded as if the names were ones he'd recognised. He might have read a Peter Cheyney once, but he couldn't be sure. Lemmy Caution, was that the character's name?

'These pages, they're typed, I imagine?'

'Yes.'

'Doesn't that make it more difficult to prove they were written by Pierce himself?'

'It would. But in this case roughly a third of the pages I've seen have corrections and revisions inserted by hand.'

'Pierce's hand?'

'Either that or a very accurate copy.'

'Presumably you can check…'

'We can bring in experts, certainly, to testify as to the validity or otherwise of the handwriting, analyse the ink if need be, the age and weight of the paper and so on…'

'And still not be satisfied?'

'There are other issues, less easy to determine. The provenance of the manuscript, for instance; whether the person wishing to sell it is the rightful owner. Added to which the fact that, so far, I have only that person's assurance that the remainder of the manuscript actually exists and is in her hands.'

'Her?'

'Alexandra Pierce, the youngest daughter. Younger by quite a long way. Pierce must have been well into his fifties when she was born.'

'And she came to you directly, this Alexandra?'

'Yes. I've acted for the family in the past. Some papers of her father's that were placed with an American university. Letters, mainly. Page proofs of a rare early chapbook. Even so, with something like this which could, if authenticated, command a good deal of money, the more usual path would be to sell it at auction; instead of which Alexandra has suggested I should find a buyer without resorting to the open market.'

'Did she give a reason for wanting to go down that route?'

'As I understand it, she wants to avoid a lot of rigmarole, a lot of fuss. It would be easier, she thinks, more straightforward to deal with me directly instead. Someone she knows she could trust.'

Kiley shifted his chair back a notch. 'It sounds as if that trust doesn't necessarily run both ways.'

'Let's just say Alexandra's not the most straightforward of people. Contradictory, you might call her. Impulsive. Not easy to read.'

'And that's what you'd like me to do? A little close reading? Somewhere between the lines?'

Pike smiled. 'Any financial losses aside, in this profession what I can least afford to lose is my reputation. If my personal situation were different, there are steps I would take to ensure, as far as is possible, that what I'm being offered is the real thing. As it is...' He prodded the sides of his wheelchair. 'I need someone to be my legs for me. Eyes and ears, too.'

'I understand.'

'Good. And the sooner you can become involved the better. Word about Pierce's supposed foray into sensational fiction is bound to leak out sooner or later. Rumours of that kind, they're the pornography of the rare book trade. The first chapters of Plath's follow-up to *The Bell Jar* that mysteriously disappeared after her suicide; the Hemingway manuscript that was in a suitcase stolen from a train; the Dashiell Hammett novel he wrote somewhere between finishing *The Thin Man* and his death twenty-five years later. We believe and don't believe in equal measure. Always hoping. If *Dead Dames Don't Sing* is legitimate I'd like to get there ahead of the pack. I just don't want to move too soon and find my head on the block.'

'I'll do what I can.'

'Thank you. Kate assured me you were most resourceful.'

Reaching into one of the desk drawers, Pike lifted out an large envelope and passed it across into Kiley's hand. 'The first fifty pages, Jack. All I've so far seen myself. Copies, of course. Enough to give you an idea of what we're dealing with.' He levered himself around from behind his desk. 'I'll see you out.'

The Passage was heaving with bargain hunters and the merely curious, a miscellany of languages rising on the air. Some old Dylan song from *Highway 61* was playing from the used vinyl store across the way. Kiley shook Pike's hand and crossed towards the alley that would take him towards Islington Green. 'If you're not doing anything later,' Kate had said, 'why don't we go to Casa Tua? My treat.'

Kate opted for the spinach green tagliatelle with porcini mushrooms and truffle oil sauce; Jack, the tortelloni stuffed with sausage and ricotta. For a short spell it was possible to believe you were in a small café in Puglia rather than one facing out towards a busy road junction on the edge of Camden Town. Experiencing a moment of self-denial, Kate said no to the hazelnut cream gnocchi for dessert and asked for a double espresso instead. Kiley did the same.

All through the meal they had steered clear of what might be termed business. Now Kate asked how the meeting with Daniel Pike had gone, what impression he'd come away with.

'Would I buy a used book from him, do you mean?'

'Something like that.'

'On balance, probably, yes. Though I might shy away from his kind of prices.'

Primed by a flurry of car horns, Kate's attention turned towards the window and the street outside, in time to see a cyclist in full gear swerve up into the pavement and avoid colliding with a 4x4 driven by a woman paying more attention to her mobile than the traffic lights ahead.

'This Alexandra Pierce,' Kiley said, 'you know her at all?'

'As a matter of fact, I do. I interviewed her a year or so back for the *Guardian Weekend*. There was a small show of her photographs at Atlas and they were reproducing some in the magazine.'

'I didn't know she was a photographer.'

'She's been a lot of things, Jack, for someone still just the right side of thirty. Model, actor, minor celebrity. I think for a while she was in a band. These last few years, in the main, she seems to have been concentrating on the photography. If you hadn't walked out on the Saul Leiter when you did, you might have met her there.'

'My loss.'

'Well, there's a chance to make up for it this Sunday. An afternoon lecture at the British Library: *Sebastian Barker, William Pierce and the Visionary Heirs of William Blake*.'

Kiley shuddered. 'Over my dead body.'

'It's okay. You don't have to go to the actual lecture. It's the reception afterwards we're interested in.'

'We?'

'Sherry and canapés, Jack. What's not to like? I'll come along, introduce you to Alexandra. She's sure to be there. After that you're on your own.'

Standing on the corner of Royal College Street and Camden Road, traffic pouring past, they kissed, then went their separate ways.

Back home, Kiley opened the bottle of ten-year-old Springbank a client had recently passed over in payment, together with a premium ticket for the Chelsea-Spurs game, twelve rows up, level with the half-way line. The match had been a bruising, bad-tempered encounter, twelve players booked, nine from Spurs, Chelsea coming back from two goals down to draw. As was always the case when Kiley watched soccer nowadays, part of the time was spent wishing he were out there on the pitch, the rest thankful that he was not. The leg that had been broken in two places in only his second game of the season for Charlton Athletic — his last as a professional and just a few days short of his thirty-first birthday — still gave him gyp when the weather turned. The whisky was much easier to take. Settled in his one easy chair, Kiley opened the envelope Daniel Pike had given him, smoothed out the pages and began to read.

It was one of those streets that seemed to run on forever: no beginning, no end. Windows peering down at me as I walked. Doors locked and barred. The only sound of footsteps were my own. As I went slowly forward, shadows appeared on either side, closing in around me until

I could barely see the ground beneath my feet or my breath upon the fetid air. And then I heard it. Cheryl's voice. Small, lonely, more than a little off key. The last time I'd seen her; the last-but-one, had been a small club in Soho, the Bouillabaisse, an after-hours hangout for musicians, wide boys, users and spades. The O of her mouth, the way her hand caressed the microphone then stroked her thigh. The breast that slipped a little too carelessly from her dress.

Cheryl.

I struggled awake, awash with sweat, breaking my recurring dream. It couldn't have been Cheryl's voice I heard, I knew that all too well. I had seen her, stretched on the slab, skin cold as the marble beneath her naked body.

Dead dames don't sing.

Arranged around a six-storey glass tower and designed by Colin St. John Wilson — an oasis of a kind between two main-line railway stations and flush almost against the heavily polluted Euston Road — the British Library houses some 170 million books, manuscripts, maps, prints and more, ranging from the world's earliest printed book, the *Diamond Sutra*, and two copies of the Magna Carta, to the manuscript of Lewis Carroll's *Alice's Adventures Under Ground*, a gift from a consortium of American bibliophiles 'in recognition of Britain's courage in facing Hitler before America came into the war.'

The nearest Kiley had got previously to the front doors had been the café in the piazza and he was disappointed to discover the lecture and ensuing reception were in the adjacent Conference Centre rather than the Library proper. Kate guided him through the crowded foyer towards the Brontë Room, where sixty or so assorted literary types were taking advantage of the opportunity to air a little superior knowledge. Giving the sherry a miss, Kiley settled for some sparkling mineral water from a previously undetected spring deep beneath the Malvern Hills and a bite-sized sliver of Serrano ham wrapped around a small finger of asparagus.

'There she is, Jack,' Kate said quietly over his shoulder.

Alexandra Pierce was wearing a sheer black shirt that hung loose over a fitted purple skirt, a pair of New Balance trainers, suede superimposed with a bright red N, on her feet. She was just turning away, glass in hand, from the man to whom she'd been talking, evidently bored with his company.

Kate moved in fast. 'Alex, hi… I don't know if you remember me?'

Alexandra swivelled round and looked at Kate with narrowed eyes.

'Remember you, sure. You spent a few thousand words making me look trivial in print. How could I forget?'

'I liked your pictures, though.'

'Yes.' A grudging smile. 'Yes, you did. And who's this?'

'This is my friend, Jack. Jack Kiley, Alexandra Pierce.'

Kiley held out his hand.

'I've heard about you. You're Kate's bit of rough.'

He pulled his hand away, untouched.

'I thought you and Jack should have a little talk,' Kate said. 'It seems you've got something in common.'

'Really? I can't begin to imagine what that might be.'

'I'll let Jack explain,' Kate said and walked away.

Something akin to a smile played at the corners of Alexandra's mouth. 'So, Jack. Do tell.'

'Your father's manuscript,' Kiley said. 'The one you're negotiating to sell. For now, let's say, in part at least, you're negotiating through me.'

She took his business card and, with barely a second glance, slipped it from sight.

At Alexandra's suggestion, they went one block east to the brasserie in the St. Pancras Grand. The price of her champagne cocktail and Kiley's bottle of craft beer would have kept a family of four in basic groceries for a week; he was careful to pocket the receipt against expenses.

'Tell me, Jack, just how long have you been in the rare book business?'

'Twenty-four hours, give or take.'

There was smudge of lipstick, faint, against the edge of her glass.

'And the other business?'

'Which business is that?'

'The detective business.'

'A lot more than twenty-four hours.'

'And do you always get your man?'

'I think that's the Mounties.'

'How about the women, Jack, do you always get those?' Her little finger grazed the back of his hand.

Like Marlowe when he first encountered Carmen in *The Big Sleep*, Kiley had to fight the inclination to tell her to grow up and behave.

'Let's talk about your father's manuscript, shall we?'

'Very well.' There was a flinty edge to her voice as she leaned away. 'What exactly do you want to know?'

'Exactly? That's easy. Is it for real? And is it yours to sell?'

'Yes, it's real. And as soon as Daniel gives me an assurance we have a deal, he can see the rest for himself. As for being mine to sell, my father's wishes were clear. Any future royalties from his published works were to be shared equally between my sister, Frederica, and myself.'

'And Frederica's quite happy for this sale to go ahead?'

'I've no idea.'

'Surely if she's entitled to a half share…?'

'She's entitled to nothing.'

'But your father's wishes…'

'Were related to his published works and published works alone.'

'And this…'

'Has never been published and most likely never will be.'

'But if it were…'

'Were, I like that, Jack. Correct use of the subjunctive. My father would have approved. A stickler for that kind of thing. Slept with a copy of *Fowler's Modern English Usage* beside the bed. But you, Jack…' The corners of her mouth hinted at a smile. 'Scholarship boy, were you? Something of the sort? Passed the eleven plus? Grammar school?'

'But if it were published?' Kiley persisted.

'If it were, we might have to look at the situation again. For the present, however, the manuscript is mine and mine alone. To do as I see fit with. And Daniel Pike's to sell as long as he shows some urgency in the matter. Otherwise I will see it's put out to auction and he can take his chances. All right, Jack? All clear now?'

Tossing back her head, she finished her cocktail in a single swallow.

'There's still the question of the manuscript itself,' Kiley said. 'Pike's not going to make a move until he's certain the rest of it actually exists.'

Alexandra smiled. 'As soon as he tells me he's prepared to go ahead, in terms mutually agreed, I'll have the remaining pages couriered round for him to examine. Until then it remains in my possession, safely under lock and key.'

She did that little thing again with her finger on the back of his hand.

'You'd be welcome to come and take a peek, Jack. Just to assure him it's all really there. Though I'll need to do a little background checking of my own beforehand. Business cards like the one you gave me, they don't prove a thing.'

Kiley wrote a name and number on a coaster and passed it across.

'Detective Chief Inspector at New Scotland Yard. He'll vouch for me. Just give him a call.'

'I'll be sure to do that,' Alexandra said, rising smoothly to her feet. 'Assuming it all checks out, I'll be in touch.'

The suggestion of a smile and she was gone, half the men in the bar turning their heads to watch her go, the other half pretending not to. Kiley stayed where he was long enough to finish his India Pale Ale then hopped on the tube a few stops north to Tufnell Park.

According to the Wikipedia page devoted to Alexandra's older sister, Frederica, for a while she'd followed in her father's poetic footsteps: a chapbook, *Silvering the Light*, published by Slow Dancer Press when she was barely out of her teens; *Instruments of the Dance*, published two years later by Enitharmon, was nominated for The Forward Prize for Best First Collection. Since then, silence. Kiley wondered if her muse had withered and died or was somewhere in hiding.

Monday morning, Frederica was in plain sight in her office on the upper floor of The Poetry Society building in central London, where she was Assistant to the Director. As offices went, Kiley thought, it was better than most. Slim volumes neatly arranged on the shelves, back issues of *The Poetry Review*, posters on the walls. A view out across the lesser streets of Covent Garden.

Frederica was taller than her sister by several inches and almost fifteen years older, sensibly dressed in a faded green button-through cardigan and beige knee-length skirt. Brown hair gathered up with black ribbon. The merest hint of make-up around the eyes.

Her handshake was quick and firm. 'I have a meeting in twelve minutes, Mister Kiley.'

He appreciated that degree of accuracy. 'Not to waste any time, then, your sister's claim…'

'To have discovered an old manuscript of my father's…'

'Precisely.'

'You've met my sister?'

'Briefly, yesterday.'

'Long enough to be in her thrall, I dare say, but not enough to learn that she's a fantasist pure and simple. If those aren't contradictions in terms. But a fantasist, Mister Kiley. Or to put it more simply, a liar. And as such so convincing that much of the time I don't suppose she knows herself what is true and what is false.'

'And the manuscript…'

'Is false. A figment of my sister's over-active imagination.'

'But fifty pages…'

'Almost certainly forged.'

'How can you be so sure?'

'Mister Kiley, I was — I am — my father's literary executor. When he knew he was dying, we sat together and went through every poem, every essay, every word he'd ever written for publication. Do you think if such a manuscript as Alexandra has described actually existed it would not, at the very least, have been mentioned?'

'Unless it was something of which he was ashamed.'

'In which case, it would have been destroyed, rather than being left for my sister to so conveniently discover when she was in need of another splurge in the limelight. To say nothing of spiking my guns exactly at the crucial moment.'

'Crucial, how?'

'A novel I've been working on for the past three years is about to be published by Faber and Faber.'

'Not a crime novel, I dare say.'

'Not, indeed. A literary novel and unashamedly so. Advance suggestions are that reviews will be more than positive, *London Review of Books*, the *TLS*. A profile in *The Times*.'

'You don't think your sister will be happy, then, to share in your good fortune?'

'I think, if you'll forgive me for saying so, the bitch would do whatever she can to prevent it. Consign me to the small print, at best.' Swivelling neatly, she scooped up a note book and a batch of files from her desk. 'If you follow me down, I can point you towards the exit.'

'It might be useful,' Kiley said on the stairs, 'if I could talk to you again.'

'I don't think so, Mister Kiley. If you're going to find out my sister's an inveterate liar, you can do so all on your own.'

Stopping only to stock up on a fresh supply of beans from the Monmouth Coffee Company shop around the corner in Covent Garden — medium roast from Guatemala, his current favourite — and then to touch base with Pike in Camden Passage, Kiley hightailed it back north and home. The moment he set foot inside the charity shop the manager beckoned him over to his cubby hole at the rear.

'What d'you want first, Jack? Good news or bad?'

'How about the good?'

'There is no good.'

'Then the bad is…'

'Terminal.'

'The charity's had notice to quit,' Kiley guessed.

'Twenty-eight days.'

'I'm sorry.'

'It gets worse. Who d'you think's taking the lease?'

'A dog's boutique? Carriers, accessories and doggie couture?'

'Worse still.'

'Not another estate agent?'

'How did you guess?'

'I'll start packing my things.'

'You never know, you might be okay.'

Kiley shook his head. 'I'm fussy about who I share space with. And besides, can you imagine the hike in rent?'

'Come with me, Jack. Back up to Yorkshire. The Calder Valley. I never should've left.'

'Not for me, I'm afraid. All that fresh air makes me giddy.'

'Suit yourself. Oh, and there's a friend of yours upstairs. I let her in. Didn't think you'd mind.'

'I didn't even know you had a key.'

'Just for emergencies. Fire and that. Fire and flood.'

Kate was seated in the easy chair, which she had moved closer to the window, a fat paperback open in her lap. 'Picked this up downstairs. *David Copperfield*. Read it?'

'Afraid not. Just look, takes two hands to hold it. No book should be that long. There's no need.'

'*War and Peace*?'

'My point exactly.'

Kate's face showed her disapproval, then changed as she sniffed the air. 'Are those fresh coffee beans in your pocket, Jack, or are you just excited to see me?'

'Just give me a few minutes.'

He headed off to the kitchen and Kate went back to her book.

The coffee, when it arrived, lived up to expectations.

'A little bird tells me you're most likely going to be on the move again soon.'

'Fresh fields, pastures new.'

'Where I am now, there's plenty room enough for two.'

'We tried that once, remember? As I recall, we both pretty much agreed it was a disaster.'

'There were reasons, Jack. That place was little bigger than a shoe cupboard. We were falling over one another all the time.'

'That was the good part.'

Kate smiled, remembering. 'Where I am now's different. Two floors up into the roof. You could have a room of your own.'

Kiley shook his head. 'This last couple of months, we've been getting along okay, don't you think?'

'Yes, I do.'

'Then let's keep it that way. For now at least.'

'Whatever you say.' Twisting her head around, she raised up her face to be kissed. Kissed back. One thing led to another. Music drifted up from below. Afternoon morphed into evening.

'I've been thinking,' Kate said. She was standing at the window, looking down at the traffic below, the people dining at the Ethiopian restaurant across the street. 'Pierce's publisher, you don't suppose he would have mentioned this novel to her, him, whichever it is?'

Kiley allowed himself a quiet grin.

'What?' Kate asked.

'For once I got there before you. Looked in on your pal, Pike, on the way here. He thought it was a good idea too. And Pierce's former publisher, it's a man. Henry. Henry Swift. I'm going down to see him tomorrow.'

'Down?'

'Deal. On the Kentish coast.'

Kate's eyes brightened. 'I'll come with you. I've a friend in Deal.'

'You've friends everywhere.'

'The forecast is good. You should remember to take your trunks.'

Kiley thought that was unlikely: the last time he'd gone swimming in the sea had been on a primary school trip to Southend when he was nine. It was too late to start again now.

For once the forecast hadn't lied. The sun at mid-morning was bright enough for Kiley to wish he'd brought sunglasses, instead of which he was forced to narrow his eyes against the light. Kate's friend turned out to be an artist named Arthur Neal, whose strong and colourful paintings Kiley had surprised himself by liking a great deal.

Leaving them to their conversation he made his way along a gently winding stretch of Georgian terraced houses and from there down onto the front. The retirement home was a few hundred metres north along the promenade, a generous-looking red brick building set back behind well-trimmed lawns. After signing in the visitors' book at the reception desk, a pleasant-faced woman in a ill-fitting uniform — part-nurse, part-warden — led him to where the former publisher was sitting at the side of the building, rug loose across his knees, eyes closed, catching the sun.

'Mister Swift… Henry… You've got a visitor.'

The old man — not so very old really, according to Google in his early eighties — opened an eye and let it fall closed. Kiley brought a folding chair over from where it was leaning against the wall and joined him.

'I thought she'd woken me up,' Swift said, 'to give me another lecture on the risks of skin cancer. Actinic keratosis. Basal cell carcinoma. Never seems to occur to them any little thing that hastens the inevitable might be welcome. Save all the trouble and expense of organising a one-way ticket to Switzerland. Assisted suicide capital of the world. What can I do for you, Mister… ?'

'Kiley. Jack Kiley.'

'Jack, then. I'm Henry.'

'William Pierce, Henry, you were his publisher?'

Swift's head swivelled slowly. 'Please don't tell me you're another mature student, cobbling together a PhD from our poetic yesterdays? The Open University has a great deal to answer for.'

'If it makes you feel happier, my last brush with formal education was a little over thirty years ago. More passed than failed but it was a close thing.'

'And now?'

'Now I'm a private detective.'

Swift gave him a quick, approving smile. 'Here to learn where the bodies are buried, no doubt.'

'Are there bodies?'

'In publishing? Quite a few. Stabbed in the back, mostly. Skeletons, by now. Metaphorical for the most part, but not all.'

'Many in Pierce's cupboard?'

'Skeletons? No more than to be expected. Savage bastards, poets.'

'Pierce included?'

Swift shrugged. 'No better, no worse than most.'

'You stuck with him, though. As a publisher, I mean.'

'And as a friend.'

'If there were any old unpublished manuscripts rattling round, you'd have known?'

Laughter rattled around Swift's chest and emerged as a rasping cough.

'That old chestnut, is it? Thought that had been done and buried years ago. William's brush with the pot-boiler trade.'

'There was a book, then? A manuscript, at least.'

Swift pulled the rug higher with an arthritic hand. 'Talk of a book, there was plenty of that. Late at night, the bottle down to its final dregs. How William was going to take on the Yanks and beat them at their own game. Jonathan Latimer. Mickey Spillane. He even had a title. Something about dames.'

'*Dead Dames Don't Sing.*'

'That's it. With a title like that, he used to say, stick the right picture on the cover and it'll sell a million. Just one problem, I used to tell him, you can't just have a cover, you've got to have a story to go with it. And he'd tell me this yarn about a jazz singer and a black G.I. who'd hung around in Soho after the war. At which point I'd say that's all very fine, but it's not enough to have that all in your head, you've got to get it down on paper. And he'd wave his hands around and say tomorrow, tomorrow, tomorrow and pour himself another drink.' Swift paused for breath. 'We all know what happens to tomorrow.'

'So it never got written, that's what you're saying?'

'Oh, some maybe. A little. A chapter or two. Nothing more. Nothing that I ever saw.'

'And he couldn't have finished the book and taken it to someone else instead? Another publisher?'

'Someone less literary, you mean? It's not impossible. There were enough to be found, bottom feeders happy to swim in the muck. Writers, too. Hacks who'd turn around a manuscript in four or five weeks, three at a push. Science fiction, westerns, fantasy, crime. 128-page paperbacks, 50,000 words. The sort of work that called for one thing William never had and that was discipline, the kind that keeps you at your desk for up to eight hours a day. Sonnets, they were more his cup of tea. Fourteen lines you could worry away at between lunch and heading off back down to the pub.'

A sudden flurry of coughing bent the older man almost double and sent Kiley inside in search of water. Swift drank in small sips and dabbed a tissue at his eyes.

'Go days practically without speaking and then when I do, this happens.' Reaching out a crippled hand, he patted Kiley gently on the knee. 'Piece of advice. Don't get fucking old. And don't take my word for any of this. There must be one of two of the old crowd still alive. Fitzrovia. Soho. The Wheatsheaf, that's where a lot of them used to congregate, Rathbone Place. Later it was the Highlander in Dean Street — changed it's name since — a lot of film people used to drink in there. Where William met her, of course, that actress he had a bit of a fling with. The one who was going to be in the movie he was sure was going be made from his novel. After it had topped the bestseller lists, of course.'

Swift shook his head.

'Bit of a fantasist, William. All right for a poet, desirable in fact; not so good when it comes to real life.'

A fantasist, Kiley thought, as he stood his chair back up against the wall: where he had heard that before?

When they met at the station, Kate had a carefully bubble-wrapped and brown-papered package, the size and thickness of a large, fat book, under one arm. He didn't ask. She'd also brought home-made scones from the Neals' kitchen and a Thermos of coffee; the flask to be returned at a later date.

'Good day?' Kiley asked.

'Lovely. You?'

'Interesting.'

At Ramsgate they changed trains, the last vestige of sun faltering gradually towards evening. The coffee was black and strong, the scones rich with butter and blackcurrant jam. Kiley thought about Henry Swift, living out his last years alone but looked after, in sight and sound of the sea. On a good day, if he screwed his eyes up tight, he would just be able to spy the coast of France. Better that, Kiley thought, than taking a flight to Switzerland and never coming back.

Alongside him, Kate was just starting chapter thirty-two of *David Copperfield: The Beginning of a Long Journey*.

Leaning across, Kiley squeezed her hand, kissed her hair.

'What's brought that on?' she asked.

Kiley grinned. 'I don't suppose there's any more coffee in that flask?'

It wasn't until they were passing through Canterbury and Kate looked up from her book long enough to admire the spire of the cathedral, that Kiley told her about his conversation with Pierce's former publisher.

'A thing with an actress,' Kate said, her interest piqued. 'I wonder who that might have been?'

'Someone who frequented The Highlander, whoever she was.'

'The Nellie Dean, as it is now.'

'I was thinking, that writer friend of yours… didn't she do a book set in Soho?'

'You mean Cathi?'

'Unsworth, yes. *Bad Penny Blues*, that what it was called?'

Kate nodded.

'Isn't she involved in some organisation that's got something to do with Soho back in the fifties? I remember you going to a talk there once.'

'The Sohemians, yes.'

'Maybe you could ask her? If she doesn't know herself, she might be able to point you at someone who does.'

'And I should do this why?'

'Because you like being Nora to my Nick?'

Kate's face broke into a smile. 'You did read that book I gave you.'

'*Thin Man*, thin book. Just about my size.'

'You said it. Now let me finish this chapter. Old Mr Peggotty is about to set off alone in search of his niece.'

'Good luck with that.'

Kiley's mobile started ringing as they were crossing the station concourse at St. Pancras. Kate brushed his cheek with hers and continued walking. Disembodied, Alexandra's voice sounded oddly childlike, a child playing dress-up.

'You checked out, Jack. Your pal at Scotland Yard.'

'So I can see your father's manuscript?'

'Maybe.'

'I thought we had a deal? My credentials are okay, I get first sight of the manuscript. Everything seems kosher, I advise Daniel accordingly.'

'Aren't you forgetting the other little matter, Jack? Part of your job description, I'm sure.'

'And what would that be?'

'Just how far am I to be trusted? In your professional judgement, that is.'

'It's an interesting question.'

'And have you arrived at any conclusion?'

'Not so far.'

'Then why don't you come round a little later? Check me for probity and, just maybe, if you're very good, see the manuscript at the same time.'

She was laughing at him, and for now he didn't care. The address she gave him was in Kensington, a short distance from the Royal Albert Hall. She was still laughing as he closed the phone.

The apartment was on the top floor of a mansion block, with views out across Kensington Gardens. High ceilings, deep rooms. Both sides of a broad hallway were hung with framed photographs Alexandra had taken: portraits of celebrities along one side, mostly from the arts: the actor, Bill Nighy, Kiley recognised; the painter Frank Auerbach — this latter only thanks to a show at Tate Britain Kate had dragged him round not once, but three times. Opposite were city shots, buildings from strange angles, distortions, odd diagonals, unsuspected patches of colour.

'You much into photography, Jack?'

'I like a good snap as much as anyone.'

Alexandra tilted back her head and laughed, the movement softening the outline of her face.

'Does anyone really go for that act, Jack?'

'Which act is that?'

'Your straight-talking, call-a-spade-a-spade, don't-waste-any-of-those highfaluting-ideas-on-me act.'

'Once in a while, yes.'

'Kate Keenan included?'

Kiley shook his head. 'Smart woman, Kate. Sees through me like glass.'

'And takes you to her bed just the same. Or so I've been led to believe. Clearly more to you, Jack, than meets the eye.' The smile was coy and knowing at the same time. 'When you've finished admiring my portfolio, come on through.'

Furniture and fittings were arranged as artfully as one of her photographs — facing settees, low table, chairs — move anything even a little to one side and the whole thing risked falling into disarray. And like her photographs the colours were mostly muted, monochrome, offset by scarlet cushions, a side wall of brightest blue.

Alexandra stood close against the window, partly silhouetted against a purple sky. She was wearing a white top that was part vest, part something else; skinny blue jeans, bare feet. There was a tattoo, indistinct, on the inside of her right arm.

'A drink, Jack?'

'Why not?'

She left the room, leaving Kiley to admire the view, and returned with two heavy-bottomed glasses and a bottle of Bushmills.

'You could try the settee, Jack, it's not as uncomfortable as it looks.'

Partly through genuine interest, Kiley asked about the photography, how and why she'd started, if she'd studied and where; whether it had been difficult at first to get her work accepted by the bigger magazines. Any counter-questions about himself, his own work, he deflected, turning the conversation back around.

Alexandra reached across and refilled his glass. The Bushmills had a slightly honeyed taste that made it seem as you were scarcely drinking alcohol at all.

'I went to see your sister,' Kiley said.

'Made you feel welcome, I'm sure.'

'She was a little formal, thinking back.'

'Stand too close, there's a good chance of getting frostbite. It's a recognised fact. Fingers first, then toes.'

'She thinks you're out to sabotage the launch of her novel.'

'As if. Besides, she's more than capable of doing that herself. Can you imagine Frederica schmoozing the press? A PR disaster of significant proportions.'

'Maybe the book will speak for itself?'

'These days, it takes a lot more than that. If she were to manoeuvre herself into a threesome with a couple of Premiership footballers, or come swinging out of the cross-gender closet, that might manage to shift a few copies, but otherwise… If she's lucky it's a couple of half-way decent reviews, a profile in the *Telegraph* no one's going to read, and, just maybe, a shot at the Booker longlist.'

'No love lost between you, would that be the right expression?'

'I could think of others.'

'As I understand it, your father appointed Frederica his executor some little time before he died. She says if any unpublished manuscript existed she would have known about it for certain.'

'Well, she would, wouldn't she? And besides, it's hardly the kind of thing he would have talked to Frederica about. He'd have been able to judge her reaction only too well, known she'd disapprove.'

'Did he ever discuss it with you?'

'Not really, no. Not in any detail. Just, you know, when he'd been drinking some time. It never occurred to me that he'd actually put in the time, committed his ideas to paper. Until I saw it with my own eyes.'

'And that was when?'

'Earlier this year. In Cornwall. Just outside St. Just. Miller's Cottage. It belonged to my mother, her side of the family. We used to go there on holiday when we were children. Sometimes my father would go down on his own, squirrel himself away whenever things got too hectic at home and he needed time and space for his poetry. It must have been where he wrote the novel as well.'

'And what? It was hidden away in a drawer somewhere?'

'The loft space. We scarcely used the cottage any more and it was falling into disrepair, so we were going to put it with an agency, rent it out. Holidays. There were things that needed doing before that could happen and Frederica reckoned she was too busy. So I went down to make an inventory, see what was worth keeping, what wanted throwing away. There'd been some kind of leak and the man

I called in to fix it went looking for a header tank in the roof. He found this bundle wrapped in sacking, tied up with string. There was a stationery box inside. A manilla folder inside that. When I turned it over, there was the title, *Dead Dames Don't Sing*. My father's name underneath. The pages inside were a little damp but nothing more. At first, I could scarcely believe it. But there it was, all sixteen chapters. Right up to THE END.'

'You read it?'

'Not then. Not right away. But later.'

'And?'

Alexandra laughed. 'Everything the title led you to expect. Desperate women and dangerous men.'

She swivelled sideways, her bare foot sliding across the top of Kiley's shoe.

'You've been very patient, Jack. You want to take a peek?'

The safe was in the bedroom, where else? The room itself oddly austere. A white duvet, barely creased. Little by way of decoration save for the portrait of Alexandra, nude, that hung above the bed.

She moved the canvas just far enough aside to expose the safe.

The manuscript was in a folder, as Alexandra had said, a label stuck to the front bearing the title and the author's name.

'You can take it out, Jack. It won't bite.'

'Shouldn't I be wearing special gloves or something?'

'Just make sure you handle with care.'

The pages were smooth like any other, what did he expect? Most of the paper was off-white, save for a section towards the end, around thirty pages, which was pale blue. The type was faint in places, as if Pierce had waited too long before changing the ribbon. Notes were scattered here and there in the margins, similar to the ones in the section Kiley had already seen; the occasional word crossed out and an alternative written in, circled where necessary and arrowed into place. All in the same recognisable hand.

'Satisfied?' Alexandra asked.

'Yes. As far as it goes.'

'You wanted to make sure the rest of the manuscript was all there. There it is.'

There was a new tightness in her voice, as if everything up to now had been just pleasant fooling around; now it was as if she were handing him his coat and ushering him out the door.

'Go and see Daniel. Tell him he's got another forty-eight hours. After that he can take his chances along with the rest.'

Kiley knew better than most when a welcome was outstayed. The night air was cold but he decided to walk back across the Park nonetheless. When he reached Marble Arch he'd pick up a cab; until then he wanted to think, clear his head. Beyond the darkness of the trees, swans glided along the Long Water of the Serpentine like ghosts.

When he went to make his report the following morning something was nagging at a corner of his mind that he couldn't shake free. The sky was overcast, busy with the prospect of rain. Daniel Pike seemed happy nonetheless, cheered by Kiley's news. All there, every page. He insisted Kiley stay for coffee and almond croissants that came, hand delivered, from a high-end bakery around the corner on Upper Street. He was more or less determined, Kiley could see, to go ahead, the chance of catching his fellow-dealers flat-footed too great an opportunity to resist.

'I'll call Alexandra later, agree terms. She can have the manuscript couriered to me here within the hour. I'll have my tame experts give it the once-over. And then it's full speed ahead.'

Seeing Kiley's face, he hesitated.

'What? You think there's something not right?'

'I don't know.'

'From what you've told me, the only possible fly in the ointment now is Frederica. There's an outside chance, if and when she learns the sale is going ahead, she might try to take out some kind of injunction against her sister. But frankly, I think that's unlikely. With her own novel coming out any day now, all her energies are going to be focussed there.'

'This actress Henry Swift mentioned,' Kiley said, 'you think that's worth following up at all?'

Pike smiled. 'I don't really think so, do you?'

Kiley shrugged. 'Your call.' He chased down the last piece of croissant with a swig of coffee and reached across to shake Pike's hand. 'I'll let you have an invoice, expenses as agreed, some time in the next few days.'

Back outside, the threat of rain seemed to have abated. The new movie about Miles Davis was playing at The Screen on the Green. Kiley wondered why he'd never really liked Davis's music as much as he probably should have. Perhaps there was simply too much? Like Dickens. All those albums; all those fat, baggy books. A man can only do what time allows.

There were two emails waiting for him when he logged back on. One was from Margaret Hamblin at her offices at Hamblin, Laker and Clarke, Solicitors, where she was a senior partner — Would Jack get back to her ASAP? He would. The other was from Derek Becker, a saxophone player who'd had the misfortune to get mixed up in one of Kiley's investigations and ended up in hospital for his troubles. *Got a gig at the Vortex, Jack, this coming Sunday. Be good to see you there.* There was nothing from Kate.

When he phoned Margaret Hamblin, her assistant said she was in a meeting and might be tied up for the remainder of the day. Just minutes later, the assistant called back. Could he meet Margaret at Grain Store by the Regent's Canal at six o'clock? He certainly could, especially if it was on her expense account and not his.

The remainder of the day was his to waste.

Waste it, he did.

Margaret was at the restaurant when he arrived, tucking into some sprouting seeds and beans with a potato wafer and a dab of miso aubergine. Hint of treats to come. There was a bottle of Sancerre open and under way. A quick glance at the menu reassured Kiley the rump of lamb was still holding its own amongst the quinoa falafels and the seaweed and vegetable dashi.

Immaculately tailored as usual, Margaret's face was showing signs of strain: too full a workload, too little sleep. Even with a willing partner, adopting a two-year-old well into your mid-forties was perhaps not a top idea. One of the potential witnesses in a court case involving a client had disappeared. Could be hiding out in Cyprus, family in Nicosia, more likely the Mile End Road.

'It's urgent, Jack.'

'Have I ever let you down?'

'Shall I count the ways?'

He thought she was quoting from something but didn't know what.

Back in his flat a couple of hours later, he poured himself a small glass of the remaining Springbank and slid *Kind of Blue* into the stereo. Maybe it wasn't too late to give Miles a serious try. Still no message from Kate. Never mind. He had yet to finish the first fifty pages of *Dead Dames Don't Sing*.

The smoke inside the club was so thick it seemed to hang in coils from the ceiling, the smell of marijuana sweet and lingering on the air. I made my way between tables busy with mainly black bodies — West Indians and former American G.I.s — faces turned expectantly towards the small semicircle of stage where a microphone stood lonely in the spotlight, a baby grand at an angle behind, lid optimistically raised.

By the time I'd found myself a seat in a corner by the side wall and ordered a gimlet, a piano player with hunched shoulders and fingers like spindles was stroking the keys. After several aimless moments, the doodling became a tune, a song the audience recognised as her song, and a desperate hush fell over the room. Then there she was. Her body cocooned in a sheath of shimmering gold that emphasised the startling whiteness of her skin, the globes of her partly exposed breasts reflecting back the light. Fingers of one hand smoothing her dress down along her thigh, with the other she reached for the microphone as tenderly, as urgently as she might reach for a lover, eased it closer to her mouth and began to sing…

As Margaret Hamblin had suspected, her reluctant witness had not strayed far from the Mile End Road, Kiley unearthing him in the back room of a greasy spoon that was trying urgently to reinvent itself as cool. Derek Becker's Vortex gig went down a storm. Kate's text, when it finally arrived, was brief and to the point: Cathi putting me in touch with a film buff from the Sohemians, expect more soon. Then this in the morning post:

A very special announcement to our clients from
Pike Fine & Rare Books

'Dead Dames Don't Sing'
by
William Pierce

The remarkable and unrecorded manuscript of an unpublished crime novel by the distinguished British poet throws a completely new light on his development as a young writer. The novel is vividly set in London's bohemian Soho in the mid-1950s and revolves around the murder of a female jazz singer who had been simultaneously involved with a saxophone player and former American G.I.

All the available evidence suggests the novel was composed in the late 1950s, when Pierce was in his mid-twenties and still to find serious recognition as a poet. The novel's survival is in the form of an unbound working manuscript, comprising 234pp on white and/or light blue typing paper of A4 (i.e. 29.7 x 21cm) Many of the pages bear Pierce's working revisions in blue ink in his identifiable hand. The typescript is housed in its original square-cut manilla folder with Pierce's holograph title of the novel formally stated in capitals on a cream label pasted to the flap. Several pages are somewhat creased and stained, and there is occasional smudging of the blue ink, but the entire text is absolutely legible.

This is a truly unique item for which we have fully confirmed provenance, having come to us directly through negotiation with a family member, and as such we are very proud to make it available for purchase to one of our valued customers. Its rarity and biographical significance would suit a high-quality and select collection of twentieth-century literary papers, and our private buyers may well recognise this as a once-in-a-lifetime opportunity, as, in all probability, will various distinguished institutions, in the U.K. or overseas.

Interested clients are most warmly invited to contact Daniel Pike at Pike Fine & Rare Books to discuss the terms of this purchase at their earliest opportunity.

So there it is, Kiley thought, done and dusted, his first venture into the world of rare books coasting to an end. Client well satisfied. Time to step away.

Kate's voice when she rang was a little ragged, as if perhaps she'd had a later night than usual, too little sleep. He didn't ask. 'The Sohemians,' she said, 'They had a meeting yesterday. This actress you're interested in, I've got a name. Yvonne Fisher.'

It rang no bells.

'Any way of contacting her?' Kiley asked.

'Ouija board? Crystal ball?'

'Dead, then?'

'Not so long ago. 2010 at the age of seventy-nine. But she had a daughter, Susan, still very much alive. It was her I spoke to. Explained your interest.'

'You think she'd talk to me?'

'I don't see why not.'

Susan Fisher was sixty and in a more forgiving light could have passed for ten years younger. Her hair, platinum blonde with a hint of silver, looked to have been recently styled and cut; her clothes, Kiley guessed, were well-chosen or expensive or both. The apartment where she lived, on the upper floor of a late-Victorian double-fronted house on the fringes of Hampstead, was comfortably furnished, rugs in muted colours on the floor, a cat — Siamese, Kiley thought — fixing him with a look of disdain from where it lay, curled, at a corner of a well-upholstered settee.

Three albums of her mother's photographs and ephemera lay ready on the dining room table.

'Tea, Mr Kiley? Coffee? Something stronger?'

'Tea would be fine, thank you. And it's Jack, please. Jack.'

'Then you must call me Susan.' She smiled. It was a nice smile. Not overwrought with meaning and secure. 'When my husband died, I went back to using my own name. Fisher. It seemed ungrateful somehow, seeing he'd left me more than comfortably off. But finding myself alone after the best part of thirty years I needed to find who I was again. No longer somebody's wife.'

'I understand.'

'Do you? Well, it's good of you to say so. Now please, do start going through those things of mother's while I attend to the tea.'

The first album was mostly family photographs. Susan, at no more than eight or nine, already recognisable as the woman she had since become; her mother, strikingly beautiful when she was younger and possessed of a vitality that shone through even the most formal of moments; a sombre-faced man Kiley presumed to be Susan's father.

The remaining albums contained a mixture of press cuttings, photos and playbills. Theatre programmes from places Kiley had heard of but never visited. Showcards from films he had never seen. Studio-shot glamour portraits in which Yvonne Fisher, wearing a skimpy swimming costume, reached up for a beach ball high above her head, or, bending low in a scoop-topped blouse, patted an obliging puppy with her hand.

'She hated all that,' Susan Fisher said, setting cups and saucers down on a tray. 'All that charm school nonsense. Pin-ups for *Picturegoer* and *Picture Show*. Signed postcards for the fans. What she wanted to do was act, not pose. But in those days, if you were an actress — a starlet, as they used to call them — it was the only way. Maybe it still is, I don't know.'

'How successful was she?' Kiley asked. 'Looking at all of this, it seems as if she worked a good deal, but I'm afraid her name didn't ring any bells.'

'It was a long time ago, Mr Kiley...'

'Jack.'

'I'm sorry, yes, Jack. All a long time ago and there are precious few names from those days, British names that is, that remain in the public consciousness. Diana Dors, I suppose. Virginia McKenna, maybe. Susan Shaw. Poor Susan — I was named after her, you know. She and my mother acted together in the first film mother made.'

Reaching past Kiley, she turned the page.

'There. *Wide Boy*. A cheap crime film, just a little over an hour long, and, as I remember it, not very good at all. Of course, Susan was the star and most of my mother's performance ended up on the cutting room floor.'

'You said poor Susan when you mentioned her before…'

'Yes. Her husband, her second husband, crashed the sports car he was driving and was killed. Susan never got over it. She started drinking, drinking heavily, and never recovered. She was penniless when she died. The studio paid for her funeral.'

'Your mother didn't follow in those footsteps, at least.'

'No. Though to hear her reminisce about those days, it wasn't as if she didn't try.'

Turning another page, she pointed at a photograph showing a youngish woman, smartly dressed but clearly more than a little tipsy, standing between two men and smiling at the camera for all she was worth.

'That was taken outside the Wheatsheaf on Rathbone Place. Practically a home from home in those days. And there, on the left, that's the man you're interested in. William Pierce.'

Kiley peered closely. Pierce was just above medium height, dark suit, cigarette, homburg hat, cockeyed smile.

'This is when they were having an affair?'

'Is that what it was? I don't know. They were close, certainly.'

'And this?' Kiley pointed at the other man. Taller, leaner of face, hat at a rakish angle, a sardonic look in his eyes.

'Anthony LeStrange. He was a writer. A screenwriter. It was Anthony who was meant to be turning William's book into the film that would be my mother's vehicle to stardom. A nightclub singer in love with two men, one white and one black. Quite daring for its day.' She shook her head. 'My mother used to laugh about it later in life: the film that was never made from the book that was never written.'

'Never? You're sure?'

'A few lines scribbled on the back of an envelope, perhaps, but other than that, I doubt it very much. And I'm sure my mother would have said if it were.' She smiled a trifle sadly, recalling her mother's pleasure. 'I think they were all too busy having a good time.'

'Come round for dinner,' Kate had said. 'Latish. Eight-thirty. Nine.' They sat in the window of Kate's apartment, the table fitting neatly into the bay. It was only the second time Kiley had been there since she'd moved in. There were still books in boxes, newspapers and magazines in overlapping piles on the floor.

'I spoke with Daniel today,' Kate said. 'He seems really pleased. Apparently he's had one or two serious offers already. Big money, too. Just as well. I see news has sneaked out on to the web. Famous poet's sexy Soho past. Be in the papers tomorrow. The broadsheets, at least.' She stopped, seeing the shift in Kiley's expression, the frown. 'What? What's the matter?'

'I just hope he's not about to fall flat on his face.'

'I thought you assured him everything was okay?'

'As far as I could tell. I offered to poke around further, but he wasn't interested. Too anxious to go ahead.'

'And you think that was a mistake?'

'I hope not. I don't know.'

'Was this something Susan Fisher said? Something to do with her mother?'

'Not really, no. Just some stupid itch that won't go away.'

'Calamine lotion, Jack. That or a good night's sleep.'

Dinner over — fillets of brill, new potatoes, broccoli, green beans — Kiley said no to a second glass of wine, stood stranded between table and door.

'Go home,' Kate said, not unkindly. 'Get some rest.'

He woke at three, a little after, seven minutes past, the time top right on the screen when he switched on the computer. Typed the name into the search bar: Anthony LeStrange. William Pierce's drinking companion, screenwriter and friend. Who was to say he hadn't turned his hand to fiction as well? There were eleven entries under his name, four of them immediately relevant: Wikipedia, IMDB, filmmakers.com, screenplaylists.com. Seven screenplays filmed between 1949 and 1962 and LeStrange was listed as co-writer on three more and an associate producer credit on two others. But nothing to suggest he'd ever turned his hand to other forms of writing, not even the shortest of short stories, an article on screenwriting for *Sight and Sound*.

Before going back to bed, Kiley went across to the window and looked down at the street outside. A young fox, lean and with a healthy brush of tail, stood stock still at the kerb edge, nose in the air, before trotting neatly across the road and disappearing out of sight.

Almost the next thing he knew was the phone going, jerking him awake. Susan Fisher's cultivated voice. 'Jack, I hope I'm not calling too early?'

'No. No, not at all.'

'It's just that I've remembered. Anthony had a brother. Christopher. I think he was some kind of a writer, too.'

Kiley thanked her, bundled out of bed, splashed water on his face and set coffee on the stove. Christopher, then. Christopher LeStrange. *LinkedIn* offered him the opportunity to view the profiles of twenty-five top professionals with that name. *PeekYou*, better still, boasted forty-three with the same name or near enough. Then there were *Facebook*, *MySpace* and *Spokeo*. Two cups of coffee later, Kiley was bowed down by information overload, disappointed and confused. If Susan Fisher had been correct in remembering Anthony's brother as a writer, he seemed to be a writer who — unless he were the Christoper LeStrange whose research area had been disorders of the lower bowel, or the LeStrange with a seemingly inexhaustible interest in the Southern India Railway companies of the 1860s — didn't seem to have published a thing.

His back was aching from sitting in the same position too long and his eyes blurry from staring at the screen. By some small miracle, Margaret Hamblin's assistant was able to put him through right away.

'A favour, Margaret… '

'Name it.'

'That whizkid of yours who can track down absolutely anything on the internet from a window seat in Starbucks…'

In only a little more time than it would take to down and digest a large Caramel Cocoa Cluster Frappuccino with layers of graham cracker crumble, the results were spooling on to Kiley's computer. Hiding behind a plethora of names, none even close to his own, it seemed that between 1957 and 1989 Christopher LeStrange had published no less than sixteen westerns, three science fiction tales, four travel books, two crime novels and fifteen stories, each sixty-four pages long, in the *Sexton Blake Library*. Born in 1935, three years after his brother, Christopher had died in 2015 at the age of eighty.

Kiley took a walk around the block to digest the news. The fact that Pierce had been close — one relative away — to a productive writer of pulp fiction meant little or nothing on its own. In the corner shop, he bought one newspaper and glanced through several others. Only two seemed to have picked up on the story of the distinguished poet's disreputable literary past, though both emphasised the potentially large sums the newly-discovered manuscript might fetch on the specialist collectors' market.

Back indoors, Kiley tried calling Daniel Pike's number, but the line seemed to be permanently engaged. Confronting Alexandra Pierce without something stronger would earn him little more than a look as disdainful as Susan Fisher's Siamese and a bored *so what?*

What was needed was another angle of attack.

Another crack in Alexandra's story.

The next two hours were spent on the phone, laptop open, calling every plumber and handyman within a fifteen-mile radius of St. Just. Penzance to Land's End. He was on the point of giving up when he finally tracked down the man who had been out, twice, to Miller's Cottage in the preceding three months. Yes, there'd been a leak. Yes, the header tank. The loft. No memory of anything up there being found, taken back down. Nothing wrapped in sacking; no kind of container, large or small. Was he sure? Course he was bloody sure.

So, now, was Kiley.

More or less.

A further call to Daniel Pike proved as fruitless as before.

Time to tackle Alexandra herself.

Early evening: the light just beginning to fade. Shadows deepening across the park. Many of the windows in the mansion block were already illuminated, some with their blinds partly closed. A couple were leaving as Kiley arrived and with a brisk word of thanks he stepped inside and crossed the tiled lobby to the lift.

The door to Alexandra's apartment was ajar.

Voices raised inside.

And then a scream.

Alexandra was crouching at the far side of the room, one arm raised as if to ward off danger, her face pale against the blue of the wall. Kiley took one cautious step towards her, then another, and her eyes flinched, staring past him, past his shoulder, Kiley turning just in time to avoid the blow aimed at the back of his head and swivelling smartly away.

He was tall, around Kiley's height, and heavier, but slow, out of condition. Kiley hit him twice in the body and he stumbled back then charged, head down, arms flailing. At the last moment, Kiley stepped aside and stuck out a leg, the impetus sending his attacker headlong into a low table, then somersaulting to the floor.

When he pushed himself up onto his hands and knees, there was blood seeping from a cut above his right eye and he was breathing heavily.

'Fuck this for a game of soldiers,' he said.

Kiley helped him to his feet.

'You know this bastard?' Alexandra said, moving warily away from the wall.

'Not exactly.'

'Steven LeStrange…'

'Jack Kiley.'

They shook hands. Alexandra muttered something coarse beneath her breath and turned away.

Some twenty minutes later, the room set to rights, a plaster rather clumsily in place over LeStrange's eye, the two men sat facing one another while Alexandra, having changed and repaired her face, uncorked a bottle of wine.

'I'm finding this,' she said, 'all a little hard to believe. One minute this oaf is calling me a mercenary bitch and threatening to kill me, the next I'm pouring him a glass of half-way decent Merlot.'

'I didn't mean it,' LeStrange said. 'The killing you part.'

'That wasn't how it seemed at the time.'

'Well, I'm sorry, okay? But you've got to admit…'

'Admit what?'

'You stitched me up. Lied to your hind teeth.'

Alexandra shrugged.

'He does have a point,' Kiley said.

'And which point is that?'

'As I understand it, when Steven was going through his father's things…'

'A nightmare. Copies of everything he'd ever written, not in any sort of order at all.'

'… he came across the manuscript of *Dead Dames Don't Sing*.'

'That's right. Along with several others which, for whatever reason, had never been published. Some with publishers' rejection letters, some not. But this particular manuscript had a letter with it which made clear it was written at your father's request. Paid for and commissioned by him and based upon his own outline, which was attached. My father delivered a first draft which your father read through, adding suggestions for some small changes before sending it back. Before those revisions could be made, for whatever reason, your father must have changed his mind about any possible publication. There was no second draft.'

Alexandra angled her face away.

'I showed you your father's letter,' LeStrange continued, 'when I first got in touch, wondering if the manuscript would have any particular value. And you said you thought probably not, though there was a faint chance it might be of interest to a PhD student somewhere researching your father's early work. Find the right person, you said, it might fetch as much as six or seven hundred pounds. Leave it with me and I'll use my contacts, ask around. Better still, why don't I just take it off your hands? And for the manuscript and the letter, you offered me five hundred pounds.'

'Which you accepted.'

'In good faith. While you thought you'd find a way to make a great deal more.'

Alexandra shrugged. 'If you were gullible, that's not exactly my fault, is it?'

'You lied.'

'That's not a crime.'

'Maybe not,' Kiley said, 'but I suspect the kind of misrepresentation you were guilty of foisting on Daniel Pike might well be.'

'Daniel believed what he wanted to believe.'

'If you'd shown him the letter as well as the manuscript, he wouldn't have been able to, would he? You've still got it, I suppose?'

'What if I've burned it?'

'Then,' LeStrange said, 'I've a photocopy and another scanned into the computer. Perhaps I'm not quite as gullible as you took me for.'

Alexandra went into the bedroom and came back with a plain A3 envelope, the letter inside.

'Take it. And get out of my house, the pair of you. If I never see either of you again, it won't be too soon.'

Like most stories that begin with 'Once upon a time..', this particular story has a happy ending. For some, at least. Daniel Pike withdrew the advertised manuscript of *Dead Dames Don't Sing* from private sale in sufficient time to keep his customers on side and avoid his integrity being besmirched. Kate contrived, some convenient time later, to place a lengthy article in the *Guardian*'s Saturday Review, in which she referred to the confusion over the novel's authorship as a footnote to the careers of two talented brothers, both of whose work had blossomed in the heady world of 1950s' bohemian Soho, the screenwriter and producer Anthony LeStrange and his brother, Christopher, a hitherto unremarked and under-appreciated writer of popular fiction.

As a consequence of this and several related pieces, a short retrospective of films written by Anthony LeStrange was shown at the

British Film Institute's South Bank cinema and Daniel Pike was able to sell the manuscript of Christopher's unpublished novel, *Dead Dames Don't Sing*, for a four-figure sum.

Frederica Pierce's novel, *An Inner Life*, was long-listed for the Man Booker Prize and there were rumours that the movie rights had been bought by Nicole Kidman. Her sister, Alexandra, set her camera aside, temporarily, in favour a return to modelling and was seen at London Fashion Week in the company of Naomi Campbell and Kate Moss.

As for Kiley, after some scrabbling around, he found an affordable studio apartment in the nether regions of Kentish Town, the building sandwiched between a hardware store and a tattoo parlour. Having given Kate a spare set of keys, ever hopeful he might come home one day and find her expectantly awaiting his arrival, he found instead, one grim late afternoon in November, that she had been and gone, leaving behind one of Arthur Neal's paintings, the one she had bought that day in Deal, a semi-abstract landscape — rich reds, dark blues and lustrous greens, all leaning, one against the other — that gladdened his heart and banished, for a time at least, all thought of the surrounding misery and gloom.

So Nice to Come Home To.

He had that Chet Baker CD somewhere still, didn't he?

For professional advice about the rare book trade, the author is grateful to Giles Bird of BAS Ltd., London N7 8NS.

Cathi Unsworth's *Bad Penny Blues* was published by Serpent's Tail in 2009. Her web site is www.cathiunsworth.co.uk

Arthur Neal's work can be viewed at www.arthurneal.co.uk

Also from Five Leaves by John Harvey:

Trouble in Mind (2007) A Resnick novella
ISBN 978-1-905512-25-6
ebook ISBN 978-1-907869-61-7

Nick's Blues (2008) Young Adult fiction
ISBN 978-1-905512-46-1
ebook ISBN 978-1-907869-43-3

Minor Key (2009) Short stories & poetry
Limited edition hardback
ISBN 978-1-905512-73-7